SINC

A Story

By

C. Schmidt

SINC

S.I.N.C

Is your life in SINC?

To my close friends and family: Thank you for the continued support. The world has become overly sensitive. I appreciate having a group of people in my corner who appreciate real talk.

– C. Schmidt

Table of Contents

S I N C

Chapter 1

THIS STORY BEGINS IN FELLINGTON WOODS, OR THE FELLS, as locals call it. A city that has changed much over the past forty years. When Lincoln was a newborn, his parents moved around to various areas near Fellington. Though, neither parent ever settled down in the heart of this city. Mostly because the area was once crime-ridden and neglected. Instead, they wanted to give Lincoln the best start possible. Sadly, the two of them fell out of love and divorced. Lincoln consequently moved as they moved.

Now in his mid-thirtles, Lincoln resides with his girlfriend Alannah, living in an area of the Fells. It seems to have been abruptly gentrified about ten years ago. Because of pre-gentrification, this area featured more blacks and those like him that are considered minorities, than it once did. But before these changes, there was still a bit of crime. Yet, there had been nothing as bad as other nearby places.

Corporations built up almost all the areas they could in Fellington, with high-rise commercial and residential buildings erected on most of every block and corner. A multilane, multi-level mixing bowl highway flowed strategically above and between most of these dwellings. Flow of traffic had changed and developed, moving above most buildings. Thus, it prevented driving incidents on the ground that involves pedestrians and cyclists.

In other areas, these same developers-built duplexes and townhomes – all clustered together to create a modestly-sized, modern metropolis. These modifications left many within the lower class struggling to stay in the city they loved. Many of them lost their homes due to raised taxes and additional costs. Others cashed in on their growth in equity and moved away. A small portion of these people stayed put, residing in poorer areas that were left untouched and unimproved.

Over time, advancements in technology and medicine, construction and media created opportunities for those who wanted it. But those who once struggled staying in the city they loved were now middle-class or even worse . . . poor. The small percentage considered wealthy used various political changes to work in their favor. Most of these people moved to the outskirts and away from the lower tax-bracket areas.

Lincoln had done okay for himself by working as a dedicated site supervisor for a growing construction company. Prior to this position, he went to school to learn various trades, and finished an associate degree in business management. Pursuing a bachelor's degree hasn't been on his mind much; although sometimes he wonders if he would need the degree to compete with other people and the growing need of technology.

For now, Lincoln was alright with working what he viewed as a regular job, keeping a track of the construction site's day-to-day activities. Currently his company was responsible for building a chain of retail stores throughout the Fells and nearby cities.

His father was good with his hands. He had included Lincoln in building and crafting things when he was young. Lincoln not only loved building things but felt obligated to do the same type of work. Thus, he has stuck with it throughout most his life.

Lincoln further considered himself an old soul and old-fashioned. Even though Lincoln was not a fan of 'too much technology' – a phrase his father has often used – Lincoln chose to work for the company because it prided itself on using human-controlled machinery. It did so in opposition to some of the larger companies who had practically automated every process by deploying artificial intelligence.

It seemed that, everywhere Lincoln looked, artificial intelligence and robotic technology was being deployed. Some of this technology included advancements like the modification to the self-driving cars, which had already been around for about twenty years. Some of these cars now can retract their wheels and hover. But in order to use this feature, the driver must use special, controlled lanes. Moreover, they must give up the control of their car to an automated driving system. Essentially, this system was a subway for cars – a system meant to cut down on vehicular deaths greatly.

It took a while for this idea and its features to get approved. In the beginning, hackers could break into the electronic control unit of some of the cars and hijack the vehicles. As expected, many drivers wanted to be able to continue to do their own driving. All this brought political push back and further delayed movement.

None of this mattered to Lincoln much, though. He had stuck with his favorite car for quite a while; a 2021 Indavi Specter IS7. A four-door, sporty sedan which had the basics he needed. Gas-powered vehicles were now hard to find and vintage. After nearly two decades, hundreds of oil changes and some improvements to the engine, Lincoln's car was still kicking. He refused to get something new, mostly because he didn't want a car note. Everything new was basically a robot on wheels.

Alannah, on the other hand, had to have the latest and greatest car. A bit younger than Lincoln and often careless with money, she prided herself to buying new things whenever possible. Every few years she would get a new leased vehicle. Lincoln didn't mind, if her portion of the bills were paid.

Money wasn't usually an issue for Lincoln and Alannah, when Alannah had steady work. But sometimes she didn't. For a while now, she has worked for herself as an independent contractor, while supporting various charities. She kind of fell into the field, because she was neither interested in traditional schooling nor had any degrees. Still, she enjoyed the work enough to start her own business.

Through her line of work, she helped charities by lobbying other businesses for money that support these charities' goals. In short, a professional funds raiser. Sometimes, finding money from a donor was challenging. So, when there was no money to find, there was not any work for her. This meant no paycheck. But she was oddly good at saving despite her spending. So, there were usually no real complaints at home about expenses.

In the beginning of their relationship, things were good for Lincoln and Alannah. They have been renting an upscale duplex unit in a gated community where many residents resided. A mixture of neighbors from various backgrounds;

mostly single people with a few couples like them. All were scattered about. A handful of the elderly wanted to stay close to an area which made them feel young.

Lincoln and Alannah's neighborhood was located not far from a retail center housing several clothing stores, bistros and eateries. A few lounges and clubs. Most of these stores were automated and self-served, having little to no employees. Merchandise within these stores was digitally tagged. An automatic scanner, located near the front entrance, tracked anything taken out by way of a digital payment card most people carried. Upon exiting the store with an item, your card was charged. However, returning an item required a more tedious review process.

The digital card combined information and encrypted it, such as driver license numbers, credit card numbers, and social security numbers. It further tracked subscriptions and membership accounts. Sometimes it will contain more financial information, dependent on the carrier's requirements. These cards could be carried physically or scanned and bonded to a cell phone's app.

Even though cash was still being used, it wasn't used as often. Lincoln was a fan of keeping a few twenties in his pocket, using the same money clip his grandfather gave him when he was small. Being the product of a wealthy family, Alannah didn't care how the money was kept. Just if it was kept and available when she wanted it.

She and Lincoln are both the only children by their respective parents and raised differently. This made their relationship both beautiful and troubled. Both liked their space; sometimes too much of it. Both could be a bit selfish. Sometimes, they could be secretive and stubborn, amongst other only child struggles.

The two met three years ago at an after party that Alannah coordinated for one of her charities. Alannah was working at the event, being the familiar face for the donors she had interfaced with and lobbied. One of these donors was the company for which Lincoln had worked. Lincoln hadn't any plans on going to this event, but he was pegged to go by his boss. His boss felt like this was an 'urban' event. Lincoln was glad that he did go afterwards.

Alannah's profile caught his attention not long after he arrived at the venue. Wearing a neatly pressed, button-down shirt and dress pants paired with hard bottom Oxfords, Lincoln studied her from afar. Moving around busily, Alannah failed to notice the tall man who had been staring at her from the distance. Her bronzed skin and long hair first captivated Lincoln. Her smile and body sealed the deal when he got a closer look. Gathering himself on what to say, he eventually introduced himself. Lincoln stammered a little, but still set the wheels in motion.

Both agreed that, after having gone on several dates, they wanted to date each other exclusively. After a little over a year of dating and while living separately, the discussion of them living together came up a few times. They ironed out their needs and desires. Lincoln and Alannah agreed to move into a new location that would benefit both their lives. It ended up being Fellington Woods.

The first year of them living together was wonderful. It was almost as if the two of them didn't argue. Their relationship had regular morning laughs while they got ready for work, and they called each other during lunch just to say hello. Lincoln enjoyed coming home to the smell of something Alannah had put in the self-cooker. Alannah enjoyed snuggling on the couch while watching reality shows after dinner. The unplanned, intense long sessions of sex and sometimes quickies. The touching of each other for no reason at all.

Life was good.

Chapter 2

6:30 A.M. LYING IN THEIR KING BED ON HER STOMACH with her head slightly under a pillow, Alannah was asleep opposite of Lincoln. Her armed was draped across the edge. Lincoln lay on his back, too, with his face pointed toward the opposite wall as he slept.

If they wanted, they could fit two people in the bed between them. They seemed to have slowly created space subconsciously, because of changes having strained their relationship.

Birds outside began chirping louder than usual. Probably because of the sounds of cars zooming by or the chatter of those walking the main street nearby. Or because of the noise from the automated trash collection system moving slowly down the street. A wheeled narrow machine arrived at each home, locking into the trash cans positioned at each house – one inside a special housing. The narrow machine grabs the housing, lifting and dumping the can's contents into a larger unit connected to it.

At seven o'clock, Lincoln and Alannah's alarm clock shines brighter on an adjacent wall. It dings in variations from a low to loud in volume. The blueish hologram clock continues to ding, blinking the current time. It causes Alannah to change her position in the bed.

"Are you going to turn it off?" Alannah asks groggily.

At first, Lincoln doesn't respond.

Tapping his arm, Alannah repeats herself.

Breathing heavily, Lincoln does his best to wake up as he rubs his eyes. "You turn it off," he says.

Annoyed, Alannah says, "Alarm off." Aggressively she pulls the comforter over her head.

But the clock continues to ding.

"Alarm off!" Alannah shouts, growing frustrated.

"It's not going to recognize your voice if you scream at it. We've been over this, Alannah."

"Ugh," Alannah moans.

Turning on his side with his back toward her, Lincoln says, "You wanted that thing. I was good with just using my phone."

Alannah tries one more time to successfully turn off the alarm before falling back asleep. Lincoln turns over on his other side and glances at Alannah for a moment. Wanting to touch her, Lincoln's eyes follow the curves of Alannah's shapely body. Her long hair draped across her neck and shoulder. The shape of her breasts, slightly hang out from her night gown. She still managed to arouse him without even trying. But as much as he wanted to get close to her this morning, he doesn't submit to his desire. He is still a bit annoyed by the argument they had the night before.

After staring at her for a few minutes, Lincoln wonders how they got to this place and why they sleep so far from each other. He gets up slowly and journeys to the bathroom. He places the tip of his index finger on the top corner of the digital, personalized toilet. Automatically it activates the settings he chose. The toilet seat warms up to just the right temperature. It could get quite warm and humid outside this time of year in the city, which meant a lot of air conditioning indoors. It further meant a very cold toilet seat the first thing in the morning. Literally freezing his ass off was something of which Lincoln wasn't a fan.

After browsing his phone, he commands the television to turn on. Like the clock, the television appears on a wall not far from the bathroom's vanity. Certain walls in the home were programmed as display units. As expected, a thin, transparent touch screen is installed on these walls.

"TV on," he says with a calm tone, wiping the sleep from his eyes.

After a short sound, the television displays. The television shows the program on the same channel on which he had left it. Several commercials aired. Commercials such as cosmetic products to help someone look more youthful, fast-food, and legal representation. New social media and dating apps. Thereafter, one of Lincoln's favorite shows came on.

Lincoln notices the time as he multitasks between browsing social media and listening to the comedy news-show for several minutes. He's late.

"Toilet flush. Rinse," he says before cleaning himself and standing. "Shower on. Water . . . a hundred degrees."

When the shower activates, it slowly awakens Alannah. She stares at the ceiling, trying to find energy to get out of bed. Alannah listens to Lincoln laughing as quietly as he could to the comedy show's anchor, who offers his perspective on the world news.

Moving like a sleepless zombie, Alannah sits up in bed. She commands the blinds to open halfway, letting light into the room. Then, she walks into the bathroom without saying anything to Lincoln. Glancing at herself in the mirror, she locks eyes with him briefly while he cleans himself in the shower.

"Hey," Alannah finally speaks.

"Hey," Lincoln responds, dryly. He turns his body to rinse the opposite side.

Walking into the toilet room, Alannah quickly covers her face. "Eww! You stink!"

"You should have waited for thirty-five . . . forty-five minutes!"

Holding her nose as she sits, Alannah becomes frustrated. "Not funny, Linc! Ugh! You are so inconsiderate. How hard is it to courtesy flush?! Or to activate the air freshener! Nobody got time to wait that long to use the damn bathroom!"

"Well, then, use the other bathroom down the hall. Or downstairs!"

"Jerk!" Alannah slams the door while she uses the bathroom. Finishing up, she gets into the large, two-person shower with Lincoln.

The shower had dual everything. It was also equipped with built-in settings to adjust water temperature and pressure. Stainless steel fixtures, heated seats in the corners, and the ability to self-clean. Refillable canisters for shower gels and shampoo and more. High-end marble shower tiles.

Alannah goes straight to her side of the shower, following her usual hygiene routine. She does not say anything more to Lincoln. Besides, he was too busy laughing at the television show.

Turning to face him, she stares at Lincoln fondly for a few seconds as she scrubs her neck and chest. She doesn't want him to see the hurt filling her eyes. She loves him deeply, but the arguments between them have become more frequent. The anger because of them lasts for too long. It was as if they had forgotten how to communicate.

Realizing he had been more into the television than into getting clean for work, Lincoln abruptly rinses. He steps out of the shower and grabs his towel out of the towel warmer. He doesn't notice one inch of Alannah's attractive, soapy body. The two of them used to get quickies in the shower, but not lately.

As Lincoln brushes his teeth and scans his outfits, he gazes out of the windows in his closet. All face the main street in which they live. Looking both ways, and then up and down the street, he notices a couple men in suits. They're talking to one of the neighbors. One of the men writes something on a small tablet, while then looking around suspiciously.

"Who are these strange dudes in suits out here? You see them before?" Lincoln tries to talk with a mouth full of toothpaste, as some of it flies from his mouth.

"What?!" Alannah says loudly. She's unable to hear Lincoln over the noise from the shower and television.

Spitting into the sink, Lincoln speaks again. "I said, 'Who are these dudes in suits out here?!' They look like cops."

"Boy, get dressed and go to work! Why are you so nosy?"

Lincoln shrugs and ponders his clothing selection. "Hey, VIDA, what is today's weather?"

The Virtual Information and Data Assistant makes a sound and replies, "Today's weather in Fellington will be a high of eighty-eight degrees, with a low of sixty-five. Precipitation is fifty percent."

Lincoln puts on his clothes. He walks briskly toward the large, digital mirror over the vanity with anti-fog technology. "It's called keeping an eye on what's ours." Checking how he looks one last time; he walks out of the bathroom.

"Whatever. You just . . . nosy." Alannah was unable to finish what she said. Lincoln abruptly left without giving her any affection. Shutting off the shower, she wraps a towel around her and goes into her closet.

Deep into her thoughts, Alannah peruses her closet. She uses her garment rotator to move her clothing around a section, as if she was running a vintage-but-modern dry cleaners. After finding what she wanted to wear and having had completed her morning routine, she dressed and left for work.

Alannah has dedicated herself to supporting charities for a while. Even though the work has been challenging, she enjoys helping others. And so, she started her own business before she met Lincoln — working as an independent contractor.

The event where she and Lincoln met was held by one of the first clients, for whom she had successfully collected several thousand dollars. But over the years, she had hit some bumps in the road. Sometimes the money she earned was unstable, and this concerned Lincoln. Moreover, she works long hours. Lincoln, on the other hand, would like her home more often.

But Lincoln works long hours as well. In fact, some days he does not get home till late. Usually, this happens when Lincoln's project manager wants to get certain tasks done ahead of time; though, he does them at the last minute when there was not any room for tasks being completed late.

Lincoln also likes to hang with his boys. Often, he meets up with them right after work for beers and some nine-ball at a local billiard. He does this a little too often for Alannah's taste, however, and that causes more friction at home. Lately, when she is home, he isn't.

Whenever they are home at the same time, there has been mostly arguments and intense quiet between them. Alannah and Lincoln argue more over little things, but the neither can figure out when it began. Although Alannah has an idea as to why, she hasn't said much about it. After all, it's a sensitive subject.

But a year and a half ago, Lincoln came home to a happy Alannah. The smile she wore on this day was so wide and bright that the sun could've taken a break. But she had news for Lincoln. Alannah knew how much he loved his snacks after work. So, she hid a pregnancy tester in the box on top of one of the snacks. As Lincoln reached for the box, the tester fell onto the counter. When Lincoln looked at it, it was as if time stood still. He was so happy to see that positive symbol on the tester, so much so in fact that he cried.

Six months later, though, Alannah had a miscarriage. This was not long after finding out that they would be having a son. Even with all the technological advancements, their baby couldn't be saved. A chromosome abnormality had been discovered in the fetus.

Alannah has been on vitamins and hormones since. She further had regular doctor visits. She hoped that, if they wanted to try again, they wouldn't go through the same thing twice. Despite this, now she felt as if Lincoln had shut down a lot emotionally. She felt as if he has neither processed his grief thoroughly, nor gotten enough help to move past it.

Both attempted therapies, but they weren't consistent. Both stopped after only a few sessions. Alannah and Lincoln felt as if they had heard enough to move forward on their own. But realistically, they had only brushed the surface. Thus, neither allowed the therapy to get to the core of their issues. They were told to be patient; however, they didn't see therapy for what it should have been: a marathon. Slow and steady. They treated it like a race.

Since then, Alannah tried to gradually change the relationship subject, hinting more at marriage. Her parents had been together for quite a while; twenty-years. After her father died suddenly, her mother eventually moved on. Alannah wanted her parents' long-term vision for herself. She wanted to grow old with Lincoln.

She and Lincoln had spoken about marriage when they were dating, but it had gotten lost in life. Between moving in together, the pregnancy and miscarriage, marriage was a distant subject. As a result, some of their relationship goals were silently put on hold.

Now, it seemed as if the relationship is on autopilot. There wasn't a clear or happy destination in sight.

Chapter 3

ANOTHER MORNING BROUGHT ABOUT THE SAME ROUTINE, with small modifications depending on the day. Lincoln sat on an ottoman in his closet, waiting on his automatic steamer to finish steaming his shirt. Once it finished, he can move onto his pants. Alannah, as if she is hypnotized, stared at her clothing rack as it rotated. She was almost sure the same clothes had passed her eyes a few times now; still, she couldn't figure out what to wear.

Make up your mind, she thinks.

Hearing the rotating device, Lincoln ponders the same. Both dress without saying much to each other for a while. Only the sounds of running water, footsteps and throat-clearing can be heard.

"What time are you coming home?"

"Dunno. I might shoot pool after work," Lincoln replies, splashing cologne on his face.

Sighing, Alannah turns to face Lincoln. "Could we have one week where you don't go out? It's like the third time this week. Sometimes I wonder . . ."

"Wonder what, A?"

Alannah shakes her head in silence.

"I already told the homies I was coming. Told Zeke I would pick him up since his car needs to charge. Can you believe he forgot to plug it in when he got home?" Saying nothing more, Lincoln walks out of the bathroom.

Shaking her head subtly, Alannah glances at the mirror and watches Lincoln leave the bathroom. Her smart wristwatch buzzes. Looking at it closely, she notices a text message from her friend Sherrie.

Hey! It's Wine-Down Wednesday! You coming after work?

Alannah continues getting ready while she thinks about the invite. She would much rather be home with Lincoln, taking small steps to rekindle their relationship. But he is going out. So, she might as well too.

Hey! Not sure. Let you know.

Alannah enjoyed hanging out with her girls, but she was also a homebody. She needed to have a delicate balance of private and social life. Therefore, she could avoid feeling overwhelmed and pushed to her limits. Sherrie was the opposite. Sherrie always had something to do and somewhere to be. Moreover, she seemed to move non-stop.

As Alannah starts toward the main floor, she paused halfway down the stairs. Briefly she thought of how she used to love the smell of coffee upon entering the kitchen. Since Lincoln normally got up and left before her during the week, he would schedule the coffee maker. He made enough for them to have during their commute to work. Lately, however, he has been frequenting the coffee stand at his company's work site.

After making herself instant coffee, Alannah grabbed her bag and tablet. She headed for the garage, using her personal identification number (PIN) to lock the door behind her. Getting in her car, she placed her index finger on a biometric reader, activating the car's engine. In response, the car dinged a few times as it booted, greeting her through a tablet-sized screen on the dashboard when it's completely activated.

Hello, Alannah. Where would you like to go this morning?

Several options appear on the screen from which Alannah can choose. *Work* is listed after *home*. Thereafter are the closest grocery store, a gym, friends' addresses and a few hang out spots.

"Work," Alannah says coldly, right before the car activates her seatbelt. She backs out of the driveway and begins her route to the I-44 expressway toward her job. She tries to relax, even though she's feeling tired, annoyed and unmotivated.

Today, Alannah chooses the special self-driving lanes. Therefore, she can get some extra sleep along the way. Perhaps she's tired because of the wild dream of which she can't seem to remember all the details. After about a ten-minute wait at the self-driving entrance, her car is automatically connected to the controlled-driving system (CDS). She is on her way.

Nearly an hour later, Alannah gets a blaring notification that her exit was approaching. The car responds to the changes, vibrating her seat enough to awaken her. It adjusts the steering wheel, putting her back into control. Once free from the CDS, Alannah drives for another few minutes. Then, she pulls into a small business park that had vintage, brick buildings. Once parked, she walks to the building and enters its main doors.

Walking deeper inside the building's lobby, Alannah notices a man sitting on a bench by the café. He's reading a digital brochure with the word SINC across the front of it. The brochure's design catches her eye. Staring, Alannah quickly looks away. But the man notices her looking when he glances up.

Alannah steps inside the nearest elevator, putting in her pin to go to the top floor. The highest floor held multiple businesses, including the current charity for whom she was lobbying. After greeting various staff, Alannah positions herself in the empty office. She was told she could use it until the position requiring this office was filled. Though since Alannah was technically not on their staff, she didn't have a permanent office.

Settling into her seat, Alannah briefly browses social media to get a laugh. Normally her friends would post silly memes that helped her get through tough workdays.

Laughter is Alannah's main method to jumpstart her day. But just as she places her phone down, someone knocks on the door.

"Yes?" Alannah says, turning on her tablet and pulling out her planner.

The door opens, and the person behind it starts speaking before they're seen. "Alannah, have a minute? We need to talk."

"Sure, Chase. What's up?"

Chase wore multiple hats for the charity – co-founder, accountant, human resources representative, mediator and other things. This small charity has made major strides in a short time.

Sighing, Chase sits. He leans on his knees. "We gotta halt your work." He rubs his heads with his hands in a stressful manner.

"Oh, no. Why?" Alannah says, concerned. She leans back into the plush office chair. Sunlight pierces through the window, draping her shoulders.

"Can't afford to pay you for your services right now."

"But I was so close to landing another account for you guys. I'm *this* close to getting them to commit fifty-K!"

"Well, if you want to do that – continue to work that angle; for free. Please, be our guest. We can offer you some sort of . . . I don't know . . . funds to pay toward expenses . . . like your phone usage, mileage, etc. But we can't pay you your normal rate. Not until more money comes in soon. A lot more than fifty thousand. So sorry, A. Think about it. I'm sacrificing some of my own salary right now to keep things afloat." Before Alannah could say anything more, Chase gets up and leaves.

Waiting a few minutes to gather her thoughts, Alannah collects her things and leaves. She sits in her car for a few minutes, staring out of the window. She wants to cry but refuses. So, she dials Lincoln instead. The call goes to his voicemail.

Taking a moment to get her mind together, she leaves the parking lot. Alannah takes another route home, stopping by a grocery store along the way. This grocery store wasn't the usual one she frequented. In fact, going food shopping at all was a scarce action for her. Most of the goods she and Lincoln needed could be ordered directly from the household fridge.

Approaching the store's large parking lot, Alannah's phone rings. It comes through the Bluesphere connection in her car — a new and fast technology that replaced traditional Bluetooth technology several years before.

"Hey, girl," Alannah says, after seeing Elina's name appear on the car's dashboard.

"Heyyyy. How's work?"

Alannah sighs. "I need a drink, Elina. A nice tall one." She watches the store's various patrons go in and out.

"That bad, huh?" Elina replies. "Well, it sounds like you need to bring your butt out tonight."

"I might. I'm about to run into this store. Can I call you back?"

"Of course!"

After hanging up, Alannah sits for a few more minutes. She observes the people nearby. Various patrons, like families and people, seem happy. Walking inside the store, a machine at the entrance asks Alannah if she would like a cart. If so, Alannah must select the size. Pressing 'small' on the screen, the machine makes a brief noise. A small plastic cart exits through the side of it. Someone leaving the nearest check-out station pushes their larger cart with wheels to a nearby rack. The machine grabs this cart by the wheels, sending it along a path toward others like it. It locks it into place until it's needed again.

Alannah casually strolls around the store but doesn't notice she is being watched. A tall, brown-skinned, athletically built man watches her closely as he digitally inventories products nearby. Based on his clothing – a neatly pressed button up shirt and khaki pants - he appears to be a manager of the store. He scans a barcode at the end of each shelf, which calculates the shelf's inventory. It tracks each item's weight, along with special sensors built into the packaging.

He is one of the only three physical on-site employees. Almost every item is processed digitally through the automated check-out. So, there is no need for cashiers. Besides inventorying, he is mostly there for customer interface if there are any issues. The other on-site employees are mostly there for security surveillance.

Intrigued by Alannah, the manager pretends to rescan certain areas he has already inventoried. Therefore, he can keep her in his line of sight. He is so intrigued and attracted that he can't break his gaze. Becoming distracted by a customer who tugs on him with a question, the manager doesn't notice Alannah again until she has begun to exit the store.

Later that evening, Lincoln decides to come home right after work. He was too tired to shoot pool since work was busier than usual. So, he drags himself inside their home. Lincoln is visibly tired from ten hours of yelling over loud machinery. Some Honey Jack Whiskey, wings and fries, and televised basketball would do him justice right now.

"Thought you were shooting pool?" Alannah asks, entering the kitchen.

Reaching for a utensil, Lincoln pauses. "Not now, Alannah."

"It was just a question. Damn."

"Why you all dressed up?"

"I'm not dressed up, Lincoln. Just something comfortable for wine with the girls." Alannah scans her attire, wiping off a small piece of lint from her chest. Her jeans hugged her ass and thighs like a fresh fitted sheet.

"Mmm hmm."

"What?"

Lincoln turns his back and begins peeling potatoes. "Nothing. But I did get some alerts from the alarm earlier. Did you come home early from work?"

Alannah stops in her tracks as she moves around the kitchen. She's searching for things she needed before leaving. She isn't sure how to respond to Lincoln's question. The truth would cause a fight now, but a lie would cause a fight later. "I did come home early. They needed my office. Finished out the day here."

"Land any of those new donors yet?"

"I'm getting close!"

Lincoln grabs some Old Bay seasoning from the cabinet, returning to the bowl of peeled potatoes. "That's cool." The knife he had been using hung slightly off the counter. Bumping into it, he causes it to slide. He cuts his hand when he catches it on its sharp end as it leaves the counter. "AH, SHIT!"

"LINCOLN! I don't know why you like manual labor." Alannah quickly walks over to a glass cabinet. A screen on the cabinet illuminates when she stands in front of it, showing a list of all the in-stock first-aid items that they have.

Selecting a first-aid spray from the menu, the can is dispersed, in a similar fashion to a soda machine. Alannah uncaps the spray and grabs Lincoln's hand aggressively. Quickly she sprays the can's contents on his cut. A webbed, band-aid type covering covers the wound after a few seconds. The covering blends in a few minutes later, reconnecting Lincoln's skin and sealing his wound.

Looking at Lincoln, Alannah says, "Why don't you just put the potatoes in the self-cooker? Let the machine - we pay good money for - make the fries for you."

"I'm not letting that thing spoil me like it has you." Lincoln continues to move around the kitchen. "Aren't you late?"

Alannah rolls her eyes, leaving without saying anything.

Chapter 4

A NEW MORNING, BUT THE SAME GENERAL EMOTIONS. Lincoln awoke well before the alarm was supposed to go off. He had a weird dream about something holding him down. A large object appeared on his chest that he couldn't quite make out. When he fought with the object in the dream, it abruptly awoke him and caused him to forget what happened. He realized he had been grabbing at his chest in his sleep, so much so that he tore his tank top.

Catching his breath, he became annoyed after looking over at Alannah. She is sound asleep. He went to bed feeling irritated, but even rest couldn't keep him from thinking about his issues again. Alannah had complained about him going out; though when he decided not to go anywhere, she went out. He grows angry again thinking more about it. So, he gets up earlier than usual, showers and dresses for work, and quietly slips out the house.

Arriving to his job site before most of his team, one of the project assistants notices him alone at the coffee stand. Scrolling through the beverage options on a wide, digital screen, Lincoln couldn't make up his mind over what he wanted.

"Wow! What's the occasion?" the assistant says, walking up behind him.

Her perfume reached Lincoln's nose before she did. A light and sweet citrus scent. "Hmm? Oh - uh," Lincoln startles, getting a little nervous. "Couldn't sleep. You?"

The pretty, curvy assistant leaned across Lincoln to grab a napkin. It caused her cleavage to show at the top of her blouse. "Lincoln, you know I am here before you every day. I work out early and get in early so I can get out early. Work hard; play a *whole* lot harder." She tugs at Lincoln's collar flirtatiously.

"Oh . . . cool. That's dope."

"You work out?" the assistant asks, reaching out to gently squeeze Lincoln's bicep. "You should join me."

"Um," Lincoln looks down at his watch. It was one of his favorites Alannah had given him for his birthday. "Sorry, gotta run. No point in getting in early if I am not actually working. Feel me? Maybe we can chat later. Have a good one."

"Mmm'kay." The assistant bites her bottom lip, watching Lincoln walk away.

The workday goes as usual for Lincoln, except for the erection he had briefly from the short exchange with the assistant. She was around five years younger than Alannah. She had a tighter body, and she was much more aggressive in her pursuit toward getting close to Lincoln. Her advances seem to get more blatant any time they bump into one another at work.

After he's moved past his impure thoughts, he got some reports done before his team arrived. The day went as normal, and he managed to get home earlier. Thus, he could relax before going out to shoot pool.

Meanwhile, Alannah had pretended to work from home when Lincoln was at work. She still completed things she normally did for work, but not as much without on-site resources. She was still trying to figure out how to tell Lincoln about the work stoppage, or if she should tell him at all. And it was too soon to get an update from Chase at the office.

All she needed to do was to land one more financial donor. Then, she would be set for several more months. She had experienced pauses in work before; however, they never lasted more than a few days to a few weeks.

Several hours later, Alannah and Lincoln are at home. Alannah subtly bounces her leg while sitting on a stool in the kitchen, browsing social media. "Aww. Look at them. Lincoln!"

Lincoln is stretched across the couch, watching sports highlights on the television. He lifts his head a little to peek over the top of the couch. "Huh?"

"Guess what? You know Andre and Marie? Monica's friends?"

"No, why?" Lincoln lays back down.

"They are engaged."

Lincoln isn't enthused. "Oh, word? That's cool."

"Mmm hmm." Alannah comes over and stands near the couch, still scrolling through photos.

"Good for them."

"That ring would sure look exquisite on my finger." Alannah holds out her hand, wiggling her ring finger.

Lincoln doesn't respond to her but yells abruptly to one of the sports highlights on television. "Oh shit! Did you see that?! That was a bullshit call!"

Sighing, Alannah walks away.

"Hey, can you reorder some whiskey? We are getting low. Thanks." Lincoln changes the subject.

"Order it yourself."

"But you're going right by the fridge!"

Lincoln's comments are met by Alannah's footsteps traveling up the stairs.

Liquor stores have become sparser as a result of the city government trying to reduce crime, drunk driving and the overall quality of life. With a valid driver's license and a specific automated refrigerator brand, most alcohol could be ordered via a built-in dispensary. Liquor could be ordered and immediately refilled if the selection was available, if there was an approved of-age identification card in the system. The dispensary limits the amount of alcohol that can be ordered at one time; moreover, the frequency of orders is restricted by the week and month. Patrons further need a special code to complete all orders.

During a commercial break, Lincoln scrolls through his phone. Though he becomes distracted when a commercial about SINCs displays on the television. This commercial is one of several, but this one is shorter and simpler than the others.

There is a man enjoying various things about his life. He enjoys hanging out at the beach, jogging, and eating at a restaurant. Even though the commercial never shows who the man is with, gradually the camera pans out more and more. It shows a digital eye. Then, there's the face of a beautiful woman. It was as if the woman's eye was watching the man enjoy his life. Slowly a slogan appears on the screen in sleek, modern lettering: IS YOUR LIFE IN SINC?

Lincoln finds himself briefly in awe by the commercial. Although quickly he goes back to scrolling on his phone. An alert causes his phone to buzz.

Now upstairs, Alannah is in the bathroom applying a moisturizing mask to her face. Moments later, her phone also buzzes.

"Alannah! Your girl is walking up the steps!"

Alannah looks at her wristwatch and notices the security motion alert. Seconds later, the doorbell chimes. Coming downstairs, Alannah looks over at Lincoln. He hasn't moved an inch. "You couldn't get up and get the door?"

"That's *your* friend."

The doorbell goes off again. Alannah waves her hand across a biometric reader beside the door. A latch clicks and the door begins to move.

"Hey girl! What you doing here?" Alannah says before the door completely slides open. "How you get through the gate without using the code I gave you?"

"Hey, A. I sped through behind the dude in front of me. Almost messed my car up too. Shh." Elina replies. "I was running some errands. So, thought I would surprise you. Clearly I have by looking at that." Elina points at Alannah's face.

"Oh, shut up!"

"Here you go," Elina hands Alannah a long, slim gift bag. Inside was a bottle of wine.

"Thanks, Elina. Wow. This is nice." Alannah studies the bottle. "Lincoln, how about some wine instead?"

Lincoln holds his hand up and points his thumb down.

"Y'all still going through it?" Elina whispers, leaning toward Alannah.

Alannah cocks her head to the side a bit, to which she gives Elina a deflated expression.

Shaking her head, Elina says, "Anyway. Y'all heard about the break-ins?"

"What break-ins?!" Lincoln hops off the couch like something yanked him up. He storms into the kitchen, grabbing Alannah's new bottle of wine from her hands. He then puts it into the automated wine-bottle opener on the counter, pours himself a glass and begins drinking from it while reading the wine label the entire time. "Wow. Fifteen percent ABV. Nice."

Alannah folds her arms and clears her throat.

"Oh, my bad. I changed my mind," Lincoln says, noticing Alannah's body language.

Shaking her head, Elina chuckles. "You are a mess, Lincoln. But, um, someone near the gate flagged me down. At first, I thought that I could be in trouble for speeding through the gate, but I wasn't. Instead, they insisted that I be careful due to all the break-ins. Can you believe that? With all these fancy improvements around this city - and that tall ass gate y'all got out front - we still gotta steal shit from each other?"

Walking around the kitchen, Lincoln says, "No matter how much the world moves forward, there are still some who are left behind. And they need help. But what do you do when you can't get help?"

"I guess you gotta take it," Elina says.

Lincoln points at Elina.

"But that's horrible," Elina continues.

Pouring herself and Elina a glass of wine, Alannah chimes in. "Whatever. Someone's just greedy and wants somebody's shit."

"This is why we need a gun. Old-school and traditional protection. None of that fancy . . . robotic shit they offer now." Lincoln says.

Alannah sighs heavily. "No, we don't, Lincoln. We are just fine. There are better ways to protect ourselves than a gun."

"Like?" Lincoln's eyebrows raise.

Alannah shrugs. "Oh, I don't know. Like a dog, maybe? A good guard dog."

"NOPE! Too much work! And dogs are like kids!"

Alannah pauses, wanting to say more. Her body tenses.

Noticing how awkward things were getting, Elina's laughter makes light of the discussion.

Lincoln and Alannah hadn't known about the break-ins, probably because of being consumed by their own relationship issues.

"A gun is easier to manage. I already know the type I want, too," Lincoln adds, motioning his hands like he is firing a gun.

"NO GUNS, LINCOLN!"

Chapter 5

DESPITE HER BEST JUDGEMENT, ALANNAH GOES INTO THE office – even after hearing of the funding issue. Commuting to work costs her time and money, probably more than what the organization can pay. Still, it would look suspicious to Lincoln if Alannah stayed home for too long when she was supposed to be at work. Lincoln was a bit old-fashioned and frugal; so, every penny mattered.

Once at the office, Alannah informs Chase she would work for free. All the while, Alannah hoped that he would later recognize her efforts. She managed to negotiate a bonus, should she land the donors that she said she would.

During lunch, she normally would go around the corner from the office. Alannah enjoyed going to a bistro and getting a salad. She would do her best to sit in the same area each time, since it had a sidewalk view and the park across the street. Often, she liked watching families relax and play in the park.

However, she couldn't help but be distracted. Two women, both seated not too far from her, were having a conversation.

"Can you believe that Cheryl actually tried it?" the first woman says.

The second woman interrupts the first woman. "I know, right? She said she would never – NEVER – be caught in bed with a SINC. But look at her!"

"Now she loves it! Can't stop talking about that thing!"

Looking over her shoulder briefly, Alannah clears her throat uncomfortably. She's annoyed by how loud the two women were talking.

The women give Alannah a brief stare, but then lower their conversation to a whisper.

Alannah considers her relationship with Lincoln. Where did they go wrong? Something had thrown their relationship off balance, but it wasn't just the miscarriage's uncontrollable events. She couldn't figure out what it was. They started off so well. But they barely talked to each other now. In this case, arguing and nitpicking didn't count. They also hadn't had sex much at all in a while.

Lincoln didn't seem as ambitious about life as he had been upon meeting Alannah. He neither wanted to marry her nor desired to marry at all now. In fact, money was becoming more problematic month after month. *Was he using things as an excuse to commit on a higher level?* Alannah wondered.

Alannah's thoughts are interrupted as a couple and their child walk by. Suddenly, she begins to cry quietly. A few tears fall gently down her face. She tries to contain herself, using a napkin to wipe the tears. But then, she abruptly leaves the store upon realizing she can't control her emotions. She pays for the check using her phone, and then walks to her car.

Later that evening, Alannah arrives home. Lincoln comes in shortly after her, showers and changes for his outing with the fellas. Other than quick hellos, neither say much.

Lincoln also doesn't notice how somber Alannah looks, as she laid curled up on the couch.

"Be back later," he says, moving around the home briskly.

The mood in which Alannah finds herself causes her to not respond.

After Lincoln leaves, Alannah uses her phone to log into one of her bank accounts – one of which Lincoln knew nothing about. She opened the account when it appeared as if she and Lincoln were going to split up. They could have ended their relationship. So, she put away money just in case she needed to move out in a hurry.

Within the account was money she received as a bonus, acquired from one of her previous charity jobs. She had invested most of the money with a financial advisor, giving them limited control over the account. The money has grown substantially; so much so, in fact, that she could borrow from it during work hardships like what she is enduring.

But since she had been having her doubts about their relationship for a while, Alannah never told Lincoln about the account. Moreover, even though Lincoln was frugal, he wasn't great with money. He didn't want to blend finances, so she didn't think telling him about the account was important. If she paid the bills she agreed to pay, he was fine.

While scrolling through her statements, Alannah's phone rings.

"What up! What up! What up, A?!"

"Not a damn thing, Sherrie. What you up to?" Alannah places her cell phone on speaker. She continues scrolling through her financial records, staring at the screen as if she is hypnotized.

"You sound weird. You okay?"

Alannah sighs.

"You and Lincoln still arguing?" Sherrie asks.

Alannah sucks her teeth. "It's not just the arguing. We just aren't on the same page right now. About anything."

"Maybe y'all should go back to therapy. Did you think about that?"

"Yeah. We just might have to."

"Well, come out and get some . . . *drink* therapy. Cause I know you home alone and want some company!"

Turning over on her back, Alannah stares at the ceiling. "Ugh. Yeah . . . okay. Let me get me myself together. I will call you in a few."

By this time, Lincoln had arrived at the pool hall. He was ready for a good nine-ball game, wings and drinks. Playing pool was one of his favorite things to do several times a week. Pulling up to the parking lot, he scans his ID on a screen. Seconds later, the gate to the area is opened. He pulls his car in further and parks at an available spot.

Inhaling on an e-cigarette, Tommy is outside waiting on Lincoln. He has been Lincoln's friend since grade school. Now, Tommy teaches high school students. He stands there, pulling on artificial nicotine to calm his nerves.

"Bout time you showed up!" Tommy says, hearing Lincoln's car door shut. He casually scrolls through his phone, looking up every so often.

Checking his clothing in the side-view mirrors just before they go in, Lincoln casually strolls toward Tommy. "My bad, man. Took a minute to get out of the house."

"Mmm, I see."

"Don't even start," Lincoln says, looking around. "Where is Zeke and Jake?"

"Inside. Zeke saw a couple things walk in which interested him. He made Jake play wing-man."

"Sure fail."

"Ha! Yeah! Especially if Jake starts talking his shit."

Zeke was one of Lincoln's other friends, whom he'd met during his college years. Although Zeke never finished his schooling, he found his niche in law enforcement. Then, he later worked in private investigations. He further does background investigations for various government and commercial agencies.

Lincoln briefly worked with Jacob – or Jake – right after college. Both clicked because of their mutual love of hip-hop music. Jacob went to concerts so much that he became friends with promoters. They would give Jake free tickets to which he would share with Lincoln whenever possible. As Jake grew older, he became more religious and opinionated, and was often hard to be around.

When Lincoln opened the pool hall's door, scents of old wood, musty carpets, salty food, beer, and lust all hit him. A sought out, well known vintage and black-owned business. The pool hall's been relatively untouched by modern improvements, by choice of the management. The air was clogged with colognes, odd perfumes, and body odors.

Lincoln loved it. He felt free. This place made him feel more like a man than the scented candles and funny-named plants at home. Here, he was free of anything feminine. Except for the various women working for the venue, women would come to shoot pool or patron the bar.

Pool tables filled almost every floor space, aside from the bar seating and tables centric to the room. Various tables were positioned nearby. Waitresses wore skimpy shirts and tight shorts. Their fishnet stockings moved quickly throughout the venue.

While sitting at a nearby table, Lincoln waved his hand over a barcode. An automated menu displayed in the center of the table. "I'm going to order the sticks and the rack so we can get busy."

"Cool. I'm heading to the bar. What you want?" Tommy asked.

"Whiskey, neat. And tell them jokers to come on. Those shorties don't want no part of them. They're here to hustle. Not trying to see those dudes naked when they lose."

Tommy laughed and walked away.

Moments later, a boisterous voice fills the area where Lincoln sits. "WHAT UP, LINC?!" Zeke shouts, walking over. "We missed you last week."

"Yeah, man. Seems I've been coming out here too often. Need to keep the misses happy. Feel me?"

"I hear ya, fam."

Tommy returns, carrying a tray of drinks. Closely behind him is Jacob. Everyone greets one another, grabs their respective drinks and toasts and enjoys.

Suddenly, a waitress hurryingly walks by. She is short, cute and heavy on the backside. All eyes were on her hips' movements.

Staring, Jacob strokes his chin hairs. "And the Lord created all that was thick and mighty. Amen."

"Man, if you don't bring your ass on … let's shoot." Zeke says.

After sharing a laugh, the group commences shooting pool. Lincoln finds himself staring at the nearest television while waiting to shoot, just as another SINC commercial airs. This commercial is a bit more detailed than the one he had seen before.

The commercial starts by giving a wide view of an attractive, shapely woman with caramel skin and long hair. She's standing and wearing a well-fitted dress. Her body slowly turns on a platform – like a car in a showroom - as the camera gradually centers on her face.

Eventually the camera stops on the woman's face once the platform stops moving. Only then does it show a close-up of her eyes. Subtle blinking lights move around the woman's pupils in a circular fashion. Subtle, smooth electronic music plays in the background. A phrase is shown at the end of the commercial: SINCRONIZE YOUR NEEDS.

"Now, you see? Who in the hell wants an artificial woman?" Tommy says as he stares at the television, startling Lincoln.

Zeke takes a sip of his drink. "I've enjoyed some fake tits before. Not bad. Not bad at all."

"Not bad if they are done right," Lincoln chimes in.

"True," Jake agrees.

"There is a difference between silicone and that," Tommy points at the screen. "That – is a whole person."

"Quite unnatural. Not what God wants of us," Jake chimes in, sipping his beer. "Thou shalt not worship artificial booty."

"If God didn't want us to have it, he wouldn't have given us the intelligence and the resources to make it. Besides, how do you know that waitress ain't one of those robots?" Zeke says.

Jake shakes his head in disbelief. "That there was made by God himself. I can tell by the jiggle."

"Man, get outta here," Zeke says.

Shaking his head, Lincoln focuses on his next shot and sinks it.

"Got dammit, Linc! Won again," Tommy says. "I need to be paying attention to the table instead of this ass walking around."

The pool table makes noises while adjusting the balls for re-racking.

"Don't use God's name in vain!" Jake says, turning his attention to another waitress. He follows behind her. "Hey, baby. Damn you fine. Lemme holler at you."

Chuckling a bit, Tommy replies, "I said 'got,' fool. Not God."

Twenty minutes away, Alannah sits silently with her friends. Sherrie, Elina and Monica speak about various things – all which sound like garbled words and sounds. Alannah is too consumed with her life and her relationship with Lincoln to hear her friends' funny banter. When she snaps out of her daze, she scans the restaurant's three-dimensional logo displaying on the table. A holographic menu shows up in the center. She scrolls through the various options by using her index finger.

"You okay, A?" Monica asks, noticing Alannah's silence.

"Yeah; just a little hungry."

Monica readjusts herself in her seat and grabs her wine glass. "How are you and Lincoln?"

"Let's not. I came here to drink and to hear what good things y'all got going on," Alannah continues swiping through the menu.

"Okay," Monica replies.

"Girl, if you don't make a decision," Sherrie says, pressing a button to shut down the holograph.

Suddenly, a woman walks into the lounge with an interesting looking man. Both are holding hands. While the woman looks around for a table, the man seems to be doing the same. Though, he does it a bit more oddly. It was almost as if he was scanning the room subtly, versus how aggressive the woman was looking around. One of his eyes were greatly lighter than the other.

Elina elbows Sherrie, interrupting her. She nods her head toward the door, where the couple stood.

Noticing the man, Sherrie says, "Nooo, you think?"

"What?" Alannah asks, looking up.

The woman notices Sherrie and Elina staring. So, she and the man walk toward a nearby empty table. Awkwardly, the woman acknowledges Alannah and the others while walking by.

"That's gotta be one of those SINC things," Elina whispers.

"He does have an interesting walk," Monica looks at the man from head to toe. "Like that thing hang low!"

"MONICA!" Alannah aggressively whispers, trying to keep herself from laughing loudly.

"What? I'm just sayin'."

Sherrie, Elina and Monica continue whispering their theories, so much so that the woman becomes aware they were talking about her. Quietly, the woman gets up from her table to approach them.

"He's human."

"Shh, shh," Sherrie quiets the table, before turning her attention to the woman. "Pardon?"

The woman leans in some, not wanting to make a scene. "I know y'all are talking about my man. He's human. His eye – it's a different color because he has a condition. *Heterochromia iridis. Not . . .* because he is a robot. A robot could do nothing for me."

Behind her, the woman's boyfriend shakes his head embarrassingly.

"I apologize on behalf of my friends. They don't know how to act when they get the wine in 'em," Alannah interjects.

"No problem. You ladies have a good evening."

As the woman walks away confidently, Sherrie whispers, "SINC or not, he can get some of this."

Chapter 6

THE WEEKEND HAD FINALLY ARRIVED. BOTH ALANNAH and Lincoln had looked forward to it. But not because they had plans with each another. It seems as if it's been weeks, or maybe months, since they have gone on a date. At this point, the weekend meant a break from the stressful environment of work but not much for them as a couple.

Realizing they hadn't reviewed their mail in a while, Alannah decides to check it as she relaxes on their balcony. Since it was sunny outside, Alannah wanted some alone time. The balcony offered a great view of one side of their neighborhood and their city's skyline.

"Show today's mail," she says, speaking into her tablet. A prompt requiring her security information appeared, and so she typed in a security pin. After a couple of dings, all their mail addressed to them was compiled into a list. "Junk mail. Junk mail. Bill. Bill. Hmm. What's this?"

Alannah notices a letter from the rental office marked urgent. Upon opening it, the letter regarded the neighborhood's break-ins. The letter was a general notice of what happened, along with tips on how residents could stay safe. The culprits of the break-ins have not been caught.

Another letter was also attached to Alannah and Lincoln from the rental office, informing them of their yard's landscaping. A fine would be charged to them every week if their yard was not manicured soon. At one point, Lincoln enjoyed doing yard work. It made him feel good. He felt like a man doing it. But he had neglected it for a while now.

Storming inside, Alannah goes into the family room. Lincoln is laying on the couch. She stands directly in front of the television, her eyes full of frustration. Holding the tablet out so he can see the mail, she says, "They are going to fine us if we don't take care of the lawn soon."

"I will get it to it," Lincoln says, without looking up from scrolling on his phone.

"You said that weeks ago. I could have had someone do it by now."

Sighing, Lincoln replies, "I said I will get to it."

"You're being lazy, Lincoln."

"I SAID I WILL GET TO IT!" Lincoln snaps. He jumps up from the couch and goes into the kitchen, mumbling something under his breath. Thereafter, he aggressively paces.

Alannah is stunned by Lincoln's tone, so much so that she doesn't know how to respond. The brief silence grows thick in the room, almost like humidity in the air.

"Lincoln, I can't do this anymore," Alannah grows irritated, seemingly ready to boil over at how Lincoln talks to her now.

"Do what?!"

"All we do is argue! Aren't you tired of it?"

Lincoln looks at the floor, holding a cup of water in his hands. He places the cup in a juicer. It automatically blends the various flavors he selects, mixing them with the water.

He turns his back to Alannah while he scrolls through the selections.

"Lincoln, are we arguing about the chores? Like, really? It seems like we nitpick constantly . . . but the real issues we seem to never address. You haven't been the same since -"

"Don't you say it! Don't . . . don't put that in my lap again. You didn't handle any of that well either! Don't act like I am alone in how I handled it."

"I'm not saying I have been perfect, Lincoln. But at least I have been trying."

Lincoln scoffs.

"We should go back to therapy."

A buzzer on the juice-maker goes off. Grabbing his cup of flavored water and his keys, Lincoln walks toward the garage. "*You* . . . go to therapy. I'm going out."

In the garage, Lincoln frustratingly picks up and throws a lawn tool against the wall. The sound it makes hitting the wall is so loud that it echoes inside, causing Alannah to jump.

After gathering her composure awhile later, Alannah decides to get out of the house. She rides around the city with nowhere to go, including driving past a park. On her way back, she randomly stops at the local grocery store. It's not too far from where she lived. The same chain grocery store was by her job. She realized that she forgot something when she went to the store the other day.

Browsing and reviewing food items in person was a pleasure that many sacrificed with ordering food at home. Walking through stores was the one thing Alannah enjoyed doing. And now, she was in no rush to go home to more arguments.

Unbeknownst to her, the same manager from the other store was working at the one near her home. He had been assigned to quality control and inventory duty this week. That meant going to multiple stores for several days to get this done. He had spent a few days at the store by Alannah's job. Now, he was assigned to the store near her home.

While browsing the foods, Alannah unknowingly lets go of her cart and it rolls away. It knocked over some boxes that were uniquely displayed at the end of the cereal aisle. Hearing the boxes hit the floor, the manager comes over.

He is speechless that the person picking up the boxes was Alannah.

Quickly scanning her, the manager comes over to help her. "Here. Let me help you, sweetheart."

Looking up quickly, Alannah replies, "Not my name. And I can manage."

"Well, what is your name? A little help won't hurt. They need to be put up in a certain way."

Kneeling, the manager helps stack a handful of boxes at once into his arms. He places them back on the display. Once the boxes are repositioned, a digital counter at the top of the display adjusts that keeps track of the inventory.

Annoyed, Alannah sighs. She glances up at the manager now standing before her. The manager's view from Alannah's position catches her off guard. "Why does . . . uh – why does my name matter in order for you to help me?"

"Whoa, whoa! Easy. Just being friendly. And I do work here," the manager says, extending his hand.

Grabbing his hand slowly, Alannah is practically lifted onto her feet from the manager's pull. Upon standing, she notices the man's broad shoulders, large arms and white teeth. His wavy black hair was parted on the left-side like the vintage photos she had seen of her great-grandfather in the 1980's. She quickly glances into his brown eyes.

A bit flustered, Alannah replies, "Sorry. Sorry."

"Rough day?" The manager tries to maintain eye contact while smiling. He makes it hard for Alannah to look at him, since his gaze was disarming.

"Something like that. Listen, thanks. I gotta go."

As Alannah hurriedly walks away, the manager watches her from behind. Her hips' curves and the wiggle of her ass motivates him to say something more, but he can't get out what he really wanted to say. Stammering, he finally says, "Well, I hope you will return. My name is Exton if you need anything else."

Alannah waves at him awkwardly, leaving without buying anything. She's breathing rapidly, but she can't figure out why.

At the front window, Exton discreetly watches Alannah jump in her car and speed off.

During her ride home, Alannah has arrived at the conclusion that she didn't want to be home at all. Home represented a sad, negative place from which she needed a break.

"Phone," she says, speaking to the car's smart response technology.

"Who would you like to call, Alannah?" the car responds.

"Sherrie."

A few seconds later, Sherrie answers. "Hey, A. What's up?"

"Are you home?" Alannah asks dryly.

"Yeah. Why? What's wrong?"

Alannah wipes her eyes. "Can I come over?"

"Of course, girl."

After going home to get some things, Alannah leaves right after and heads towards Sherrie's neighborhood. Sherrie lives on the other side of town in a studio apartment. She is on the go constantly working as a flight attendant. Therefore, she doesn't feel as if she needs anything bigger to live in. Most of the time she is either in the air, out of the state or staying with one of the men she met while on the go.

Inside Sherrie's apartment, Alannah flops on the couch with her bag in her lap.

"Is that the booty bag? You haven't brought that thing out since . . . um, since you first met Lincoln."

Alannah slowly nods.

"Wait. Um, you plan on staying?" Sherrie asks inquisitively. She locks the door behind her. "I mean, that's fine. But I am going to be traveling soon and—"

"Sorry. Sorry. I should have asked first. Is it okay? For the night?"

Sherrie looks at her phone, quickly scrolling her schedule and checking the time. "Yeah. My next flight doesn't leave until tomorrow afternoon."

"Thanks." Alannah exhales in relief.

"That bad at home, huh?"

"Just need a breather. I won't be in your hair long. I know how you like to get down." Alannah tries to chuckle, but her giggle came out dry.

"*How I like to get down?* What does that mean?"

"Nothing."

Sherrie stares at Alannah for a moment. "Listen. You can stay here, but don't judge me, A. Just because you wanted to go and play house doesn't mean everyone around you needs to join you. I like my options. Men get on my damn nerves too much to cuff 'em long-term."

"Sorry! Sorry! I wasn't trying – Can we just change the subject?"

Sherrie tends to rotate a handful of men, never committing to a serious relationship with any of them. She neither wants kids nor wants to be married. When Alannah or any of her other friends want to talk to her about this, Sherrie shuts down the conversation defensively every time.

Alannah believes that Sherrie hasn't dealt with some of her childhood traumas that have now leaked into her adult life and relationships. She further believes that Sherrie is guarded, but Sherrie has never agreed to this.

"How long are you planning on staying away from home?" Sherrie changes the subject.

"Well, I hoped to stay here a couple of days. But if you have a flight tomorrow then, I guess, I will go back home. Elina and Monica both got their own shit going on."

"Oh, but I don't?"

"That's not what I meant, Ree. I just mean that you are not 'playing house' . . . as you so eloquently stated . . . like the rest of us."

Sherrie pours Alannah and herself a glass of water.

"I like my life, A. If you don't like it, that's on you. But I love me some me." Sherrie takes a sip of water and continues. "But anyway. I think I might have an idea for you."

"What kind of idea?"

Sherrie adjusts her legs, turning towards Alannah. "I know someone who needs a house sitter."

"Who?"

"Can't tell you that."

Alannah puts her glass down. "Why not? Gotta tell me something. How am I supposed to agree to housesitting and know nothing about the owner?"

"I hear you. You gotta just trust me that you will be okay. The most I can tell you is the person is wealthy. They work with celebrities. I don't even have direct contact with the person. I'm just a middle-woman to another middle-person."

"Wow. Working with celebrities . . . doing what?" Alannah scratches her head.

"I don't know what this person does. Something very important, though."

"Are you dating this person? Or did you date this person?"

Shaking her head, Sherrie replies, "No. And *NO* again. You already know that I meet interesting and eclectic people through my line of work. People with money and connections."

The conversation is paused when Alannah's phone rings. It's Lincoln. Quickly debating if she should answer, she ignores the call.

"Where is the house?"

Sherrie gets up and goes into her kitchen. After grabbing a bag of trail mix for her and Alannah, she returns to the couch. "In the Hills."

"Damn. In those mansions out there?"

"Yep."

"OH WOW! That sounds so cool." Alannah pauses, her mind filling with thoughts. "How much they paying?"

Leaning forward to grab a pen off her coffee table, Sherrie grabs Alannah's hand and writes a number on it. While she is writing, Alannah is drinking. When Sherrie finishes writing, Alannah looks down at her hand. She coughs uncontrollably after reading what she wrote.

"THAT MUCH!" Alannah says, excitedly. "I'm down!"

Chapter 7

UPON RETURNING HOME, LINCOLN IS SURPRISED TO SEE Alannah's car gone. He had abruptly left during their argument and driven to a nearby bar. Once there, he had some wings and a drink while people watching and staying to himself.

Despite her car being gone, he still looked around for her when he came inside the house. He was shocked she left. Normally she would send him a courtesy text when she went out, even when she was upset with him. But she didn't this time.

Sitting on the couch, he debates whether he should call her. What would he say? Should he apologize? *But apologize for what? I didn't do anything wrong*; he thinks.

Seconds later, he calls Alannah, but she doesn't answer. Frustrated that she wasn't picking up the phone, Lincoln calls again.

"Hey," Alannah says, finally answering his call.

"Damn. Why didn't you answer the phone the first time? Where are you?" Lincoln asks, annoyed.

"You called me? Oh, sorry. I didn't see the call. I'm with Sherrie. Why?" Alannah says nonchalantly. She walks into Sherrie's bathroom, closing the door behind her. Turning on the water, Alannah tries to drown her conversation.

"You didn't see the call? How is that possible? You wear that smart watch every day."

Growing frustrated, Alannah replies sternly, "I didn't see the call, Lincoln."

"Mmm, hmm. When you coming home?"

Alannah sighs. "I dunno."

"You *don't know*? What do you mean you don't know?"

"I think we need some space."

The phone goes silent for a few seconds.

"Wow," Lincoln paces around the kitchen, unsure of what to say next. "Space? Why?"

"Things are different with us. We barely talk. We argue all the time. We don't have sex like we used to. We barely say that we love each other anymore. Things are just . . . different."

Sherrie sneaks up by the bathroom door, placing her ear onto it to hear more. Her footsteps cause the floor to squeak.

Lincoln replies before Alannah can finish her statement. "So? Couples fight sometimes. It's healthy to fight sometimes. Means we still want each other."

"Mmm. Not the way we fight."

Lincoln groans. "How long are you going to be over there?"

"Just tonight, maybe. But then I am going away for a bit."

"Away? Where?"

"Sherrie! Get away from the door!" Alannah shouts, noticing a change in lighting and shadows under the crack of the door. "Sherrie knows someone who needs a house sitter."

"I wasn't listening!" Sherrie shouts, walking away.

"House sitter? Are you serious?" Lincoln chuckles, staring out of the window.

"Why is that funny?"

Lincoln doesn't say anything.

"We need the money."

"Need the money? What do you mean?!" Lincoln replies, excitedly.

"They paused my initiative at work, Lincoln. I haven't really worked in a week."

"So, wait? You lied to me?"

"I'm sorry. I thought it was only going to be a few days."

"Just come home, Alannah. You don't need to do that. We have enough money until they bring you back."

"I'm not doing this only for the money or for us. I need this time, Lincoln. For me."

"Well, I hope you don't stay away long. I love you, A."

"I will call you."

Hours later, Lincoln is practically drunk. He's had several glasses of whiskey on the rocks. He falls asleep on the couch but then awakens to a ringing phone. He quickly answers the phone, without first seeing who was calling. Accidentally he selects the video chat and projection feature instead of a voice call. This feature takes the standard video chat ability, which projects the screen into the air directly above the phone.

"Alannah?!"

"If I ever look like Alannah to you, please stop hanging out with me," Zeke says, laughing. "So, are we video chatting now? I guess that's cool."

"Oh shit. I was asleep. My bad, dude. Didn't mean to video chat."

"You look like shit, bro. You good?"

Groaning a bit, Lincoln says, "I'm alright."

"Why are you screaming for A-dog like that? Bad dream or something?"

"Dude, please stop calling her that. Makes her sound like one of the homies."

Zeke chuckles. "I forgot. My bad."

Lincoln pauses and rubs his eyes. "We had an argument. She left mad. Thought she was calling me back."

"Oh. Damn. Sorry to hear that."

"Yeah."

"At least you got a woman. In-house action. This dating shit is for the birds."

"Sometimes it's not all it's cracked up to be. Sounds like you got a new date story."

Laughing while he prepares his story, Zeke replies, "Went out with this chick last night. She was a big girl."

"So?"

"SO?! She put old photos on the dating app . . . photos when she was fit. I felt as if I was out with a weird and flipped, 'before and after' commercial. But just the BEFORE!"

"What's wrong with her being big?"

"NOTHING! I want to know what I'm getting into. No old photos. No angles. No crazy ass filters! All that shit is entrapment!"

Chuckling, Lincoln sits upright on the couch. "I hear you. But I thought these new apps force people to scan their present day faces and bodies. To help people avoid getting duped."

"Man, I guess there are ways around everything."

The next day, Alannah goes home while Lincoln is out. She gets clothes and things she will need while away housesitting. At times, Lincoln would go for a jog on the weekend. Or he was out drinking. He was out of the house and that's all Alannah needed to know. Alerts generated by their home alarm system confirmed this.

Alannah had planned this short visit, bringing Sherrie along for moral support. Sherrie's flight assignment had been pushed back a few hours. Should Lincoln be home or come home early, she hoped having Sherrie along would avoid an argument with him.

Sherrie also decided to take Alannah to the house in the Hills herself. After all, she had more time and didn't want to just tell Alannah where to go.

The house is in The Hills – short for North Marlay Hills. It's an upscale, wealthy area secluded in a somewhat wooded area. The area features large homes and mansions built atop large acre lots. In most cases, each home's closest neighbor was roughly a half mile or more away. Celebrities such as actors, film directors, singers and sports players frequent this area for privacy. Owners of large companies and other wealthy people with deep pockets are also seen throughout it.

During the ride to the Hills, the environment inside of the car was mostly awkward and quiet. Alannah still had a bunch of things about her relationship with Lincoln on her mind. She stared out the car window as if the answers to her problems were in the trees. Sherrie was still a bit bothered by Alannah's judgmental comments. Regardless, she had known Alannah for a while. Thus, Sherrie wanted the best for her. She believed Alannah wanted the best for her as well.

Upon approaching a stoplight, both Sherrie and Alannah notice a large billboard for SINCs. The advertisement featured a man and a woman dressed in sleek, casual clothing. They held their drinks as if they were toasting to the person looking at them in the ad. At the top of the ad was another slogan: SINCRONIZE YOUR LIFE.

Chuckling to herself at first, Sherrie says, "According to you, my life is a mess. You think one of those things can actually help me out?"

"You will get bored with a robot, too. Just like you always do with the men you date," Alannah says, smiling. "Besides, you like those men that order you around in bed. Those robots seem like the opposite."

"You ain't never lied!"

Both burst into laughter.

Alannah touches Sherrie's arm gently. "Listen, Ree. I'm sorry for what I said the other day. Home life has me . . . I don't know. All over the place mentally. So frustrating."

Sherrie pats Alannah's hand. "I know. I get it . . . and it's okay. You were just being honest. My lifestyle isn't for everyone. I'm good with that. It's about my happiness. People think I am not happy because I don't want to settle down, but that's far from the truth. Right now, you need to find YOUR happiness."

"True."

After an hour drive, the two begin to see less and less city. More rural and wooded areas arise. After taking a couple exits, four lanes turn into two. The homes seem to grow larger and larger before their eyes. Each home is different. Most have an elaborate and modern design. Some look to be vintage and well preserved, with modern additions having been added to them.

A few miles into this area, Sherrie begins to slow down. She approaches a large home on the left side of the highway. The rectangular home is square in design; made of mostly large windows and glass on the backside of the home. Around the home is an eight-foot, composite security fence. Behind the home are layers of hills and foliage with clusters of trees scattered about.

At the security gate, Sherrie scans her thumb on a security reader. The gate opens slowly after a beep. The home had a circular driveway with four doors leading to the side load garage. Outside one of the doors was a basic, compact car.

"That car is for you to drive - if you need to make any runs. The 'sitter-car,'" Sherrie says, motioning air-quotes with her fingers.

"Ugh," Alannah replies.

Once Sherrie parks the car, Sherrie goes to one of the side doors of the home. She scans her thumb again. The door clicks opens and she walks inside. Alannah follows behind her after grabbing her things from the car's backseat.

The home is large and cold. Not much was cozy about it except for the fireplace. Quiet and modern. Alannah randomly grabs a book from a large wall full of books. A short chirp goes off, causing a small screen to illuminate near the bookshelves.

"Oh, yeah, girl. Anytime you take a book from over there that little screen thing tells you what you took. It keeps a count like a library. Make sure you put it back." Sherrie walks toward the hallway near the kitchen. "Come here for a sec, so that I can put you into the alarm system. You gotta have your own profile to get in and out."

"Seriously? I can't just use yours?"

"Nope. That's part of the deal. The owner requires separate profiles. It won't take long to do, but it will take a minute for you to use the biometric features. It's temporary and will be deleted once you're finished staying here. If there's an emergency, just press this button here. And if you are in the car, use the emergency button on the dash."

Standing in front of the security console, Alannah scans her face and then her hand. The system then scans her thumb and index fingerprints. She enters in her own pin number, which gives her four options on how to arm and disarm the alarm system.

"Use the same PIN for the car out front. Or you can use your thumbprint. Kitchen is that away. Bedrooms are that way and that way. Basement has a movie theatre and a bunch of other shit. Everything else you can figure out on your own. I gotta skedaddle." Sherrie begins to walk to the front door. "Oh, do you want me to help you set the alarm now? Or were you going out?"

"Going out, where?" Alannah laughs. "I don't know this area."

"There are a few lounges about twenty or thirty minutes away. Kind of pricey but cool. I mean, look at where you are."

"Oh okay. Cool. But not tonight. We can set it."

After using the code Alannah chose, Sherrie helps her set the alarm. She hugs Alannah quickly, jetting out the door before the alarm went active.

Alannah goes into the kitchen. She gets a bottle of white wine from a tall, vintage wine cooler. Once it's open, she pours herself a glass and continues exploring more of the house. Slowly she walks the hallways as if she was in a museum. Exotic paintings of naked people – mostly women in various poses – are scattered on the walls.

Awestruck about the artwork, she unknowingly walks pass a SINC woman that was positioned in a completely glassed closet. She walks by the same closet more than once. The closet was slightly tinted, so the darkness of this portion of the house concealed its contents.

Though when she stands adjacent to the closet, Alannah notices the reflection of someone behind her through the art on the wall. Abruptly turning around, Alannah finally sees the SINC positioned in the glass housing. Startled, Alannah screams. She runs back down the hallway to the kitchen, dropping her wine glass onto the floor as she ducks behind the long kitchen counter.

The home alarm blares after Alannah drops and shatters the glass, since it's equipped with glass-break sensing technology. Moments later, a small robotic vacuum appears. It begins to clean up the mess, only startling Alannah more. She charges toward the front door, struggling to turn off the alarm before it rang too long. The system hadn't fully authenticated her biometrics settings, and she briefly forgot her PIN on the account of being nervous.

Suddenly, Alannah darts out the house even with the alarm going off. She scrambles to get into the car. She then presses the sleek, red button that says *Emergency*; therefore, she can call the police.

"911, is this an emergency?" the operator says.

"Yes! Yes! My name is Alannah and there's someone in my home. Well, not my home. There's someone in the home I am watching," Alannah stammers.

After a brief pause, the operator says, "Please hold, ma'am."

Almost instantly the police know what the issue is after receiving Alannah's call, and so they use GPS to narrow down Alannah's location. Apparently other house sitters experienced similar scares and called them for help.

"Ma'am, we have this home on a high false alarm list. We have gotten many calls about this before. We assure you that everything is safe inside. We have contacted the owner and have everything we need to deactivate the alarm. The alarm company has already scanned the house, and everything is fine inside."

"Really? Wow. But . . . I still don't feel comfortable."

After talking Alannah down, and further explaining that the person she saw wasn't a person at all, Alannah agrees to go back inside. Flustered, she decides to stay in the car a bit longer. She locks the doors and stares at all the home's exits which she can see. Eventually, she grows tired and leans her head on the car's window. She thinks about Lincoln. Her desire to be home is at an all-time high right now. Still, she knows that she can't. Lincoln would never take her seriously and she really does need the space. But she just wants to relax on her own couch.

To kill time, Alannah begins to browse social media. She stares at some of the old photos of her and Lincoln from a while ago when they were happy. She stares at her screen so long that she becomes sleepy, falling asleep in the car.

Chapter 8

STILL ASLEEP IN THE CAR, ALANNAH HAS TOSSED AND turned. But she never woke up enough to further analyze or contemplate going back into the house. As the sun rises, an airplane overhead and cars going by awaken her.

Without warning, two loud taps against the car window startle her. "Hey, temporary neighbor!"

Jumping, Alannah quickly ensures the doors are locked. With sleep still in her eyes, she yelps over her shoulder, "Who are you?!"

"Wakey, wakey! Sorry to startle you! I live down the road."

Alannah shrugs, unsure of how to respond.

"Can you put the window down? I promise I won't bite."

Alannah doesn't budge.

"Okay then. I noticed the lights on the car were on all night. I wanted to come up to check on things, but I got called into work. When I came back, I noticed that they were still on. It looks like you might have drained a lot of the electricity in the car."

Looking at the dash, Alannah realizes that she left the car on after her 911 call. The lightning bolt icon on the dashboard showed that it was empty.

"Shit."

"Are you able to put the window down?" the neighbor asks once more.

"I can hear you just fine with them up. I don't think there is much juice left to put it down anyway."

"Okay. Well, I live down the road. Next time you are inside, if you look, you can see my home. I didn't know my friend was gone again. Normally I would keep an eye on things around here. At any rate -"

Alannah looks through the rearview mirror of the car. "Oh, okay. Yes. I'm watching the house for a bit."

"So, I see. So, I see." The neighbor studies Alannah as if she was a case of meat at the grocery store. "Well, have a good day. And you can charge the car in the garage . . . whenever you go back inside. Not sure if you were shown how to do it. I can help you if you want."

Feeling uncomfortable, Alannah closes her shirt to hide her cleavage. "Thanks. I will manage."

"If you need anything, just swing by. I work crazy hours but I'm right down the road if ya need me." The neighbor waves as he walks away. He gets in his car and quickly speeds off, heading in the opposite direction of his home.

Closing her eyes, Alannah takes a deep breath. When she gets out of the car, she quickly realizes that the gate to the property was closed while she was in the house. Sherrie had set the alarm. *Did the gate open when I ran out? I can't remember. How did he get in here to check on me?* She thinks.

Shaking off the thoughts, and blaming them on her nerves, Alannah walks cautiously back inside the home. She first goes into the garage, connecting the car to recharge it. In awe, she stops for a moment to examine the other vehicles in the garage. She had never been into cars but could tell that three of them seemed like luxury cars. One of them looked vintage. There were a couple of motorcycles and a few ATVs.

She then opens the garage door leading into the home, tiptoeing throughout the large and intricate rooms. She looks over each room again cautiously, like a child in a haunted house. The sun now brightens almost the entire dwelling due to the large, glass windows that make up the back walls.

Working up her nerve to go to the room where the SINC was positioned, Alannah grabs a fireplace poker and holds it over her shoulder. Slowly she approaches the glass closet, where she cautiously examines the SINC more thoroughly. A security reader is installed on the front of the glass closet, requiring a pin and a thumbprint to open it.

The SINC was powered down, its head tilted low. A small blinking light behind one of its ears indicated it was charging. It stood on a small platform resembling a circular weight scale. The platform had a thick chord connected to it, which ran into a floor outlet inside the glass housing.

In awe, Alannah sits down in a chair a few feet from the glass housing. She studies the SINC and is shocked to be so close to something she had only seen primarily in television advertisements. The SINC's features and build reminded her of someone, but she couldn't figure out who.

This SINC was a different model than what Alannah had seen in the ads. It had dark brown skin and exotic, ethnic facial features. It wore only lingerie and big loop earrings. The SINC had perky breasts, and a plump, round ass. Its jet-black hair was long and flowing, laying just over its shoulders.

For Alannah, the sight of it seemed to stop time. She couldn't move or look away.

Back in the Fells, Lincoln was home dealing with his sad and frustrated emotions. He has had so much time on his hands while Alannah is gone. He dedicated most of the time to replaying their argument, amongst everything else they had been through.

Other times, he tried normal activities to keep his mind busy. Often, he would do a workout at the neighborhood gym. Preferring to run outside versus on a treadmill, he jogs around the neighborhood near the local park, which is normally filled with a plethora of women of all ages, backgrounds and builds. Some of them flirt with him from a distance, but Lincoln is too consumed in his thoughts to notice.

When he isn't working out, Lincoln is bingeing old movies or at the pool hall shooting rounds. Sometimes he goes alone. Then, he can traverse his thoughts. Nothing seems to sooth his emotional pains. Mixed emotions have his mind all over the place.

Walking by a mirror in route to the kitchen, Lincoln notices that he needs a haircut. Thinking so much about his issues lately, he realizes that he neglected a lineup. Normally Alannah would jokingly remind him that he was overdue for one. When he needed a haircut, Alannah would compare Lincoln to a funny character in a movie that she thought looked like him — a funny ritual of which Lincoln had grown fond.

He stares at himself quietly as if he was hoping for the answer to his problems with Alannah would magically appear on the mirror.

"Hey, VIDA. Schedule me a haircut, please," he says aloud.

"Your barber, Anthony, has an appointment available in thirty-five minutes. Please confirm by saying 'yes.' Or request another time by saying 'new time.'"

Thirty-five minutes? Shit. Can I make that? Lincoln thinks.

"Yes."

"Appointment scheduled."

"Is there anything else that I can help you with, Lincoln?"

Lincoln pauses. "No. That's all."

"Okay. Goodbye."

Lincoln darts out the door, speeding out of their driveway and through the neighborhood's main gate. He calls his father during his drive, who he hadn't spoken to for several days.

"Hello?"

"Pop! What you doing, Old Man?"

Clearing his throat, his father replies, "Who you callin' Old Man? Where you been, boy? I haven't heard from you."

"Yeah, I know. A lot going on."

"Mmm, hmm. Sounds like you're driving. Where you goin'?"

"Yep. Going to get a cut. You want me to come get you?" Lincoln asks.

"No, no. I don't need one right now. So, what else is going on?"

"Oh, umm – nothing, Pop. Just –"

Lincoln's Dad's voice rises, inquisitively. "Something on your mind? I can hear it in your voice."

"Lot going on right now, Pop."

"There is always something going on. It's how you respond to it that matters."

"I hear you, Pop."

"Well, find time to come visit your *old* father soon."

Hanging up the call, Lincoln finds himself just a few streets away from the barbershop. The shop was the only building in its original state. It was still unmodified or redeveloped. Corner brick and mortar stores were scarce. Most of the buildings like this had been bought and leveled, either being replaced or rebuilt to fit a more modern-looking environment. But Lincoln's father and other barbershop patrons worked together to file the necessary applications and petitions. Thus, it made the shop a historic landmark that couldn't be removed. They had cited how many entertainers, activists and leaders had visited this location, helping in the advancement and equality of black people. The shop was now a protected community asset.

The only changes the shop did experience was inside its doors. They have had further upgrades to its décor and technology but without sacrificing or removing its overall historic look and feel.

Lincoln felt completely relaxed at the barbershop. It was one of the few atmospheres he could go to outside of his father's home or the pool hall. Both places were where he felt himself. As of late, he hasn't felt much like himself, even in his own home. He could unwind at the shop, even if he said nothing at all.

Today was one of those days. Lincoln waited a few minutes to get into his barber's chair. He passed the time by listening to the random conversations about sports, racism, sex and love, and relationships.

These conversations sporadically happened, while other barbers and patrons chimed in whenever they wanted. Lincoln just so happens to be there during one of these sporadic conversation about relationships.

"There are only four things you should consider when choosing your woman. How she is in bed. How good she cooks. How she treats you when no one is looking and how she handles herself during a crisis," an older barber says.

"Nope! Nope! I gotta better one! Her cooking, her hygiene, the sex and if your momma like her," another barber chimes in.

Sounds of agreement fill the room.

A patron getting the back of his head faded interjects. Looking at the floor, he says, "Man, listen. I only got one rule."

"Which is..." the first old barber says from across the room.

"She gotta be soft."

"Soft? Like two-ply toilet paper soft? What you mean?" the second barber, cutting the man's hair, asks.

Various other barbers and patrons laugh at the second barber's comments.

"Nah, man," the patron laughs. "Soft as in open and healed from past traumas. Soft as in her nature. Soft as in knowing how to talk to me. She doesn't berate me. She doesn't talk down on me. If she needs to get her point across, she does it respectively. If she thinks I can be or do better at something, she gets her point across without making me feel like shit. But here is the kicker: you must be the equivalent of this for her for it to work. Two to tango, baby."

A hush falls over the room. Some barbers and patrons look at each other wide-eyed. Some smirk and shake their head. Others nod.

Coming around his chair to look at his client in the mirror, the original barber replies, "MAN! WHATEVER! My woman better cook well and sex the hell outta me. And she better smell good doing it! The only thing soft I need is-"

"Wait, wait! We got kids in here!" another barber interjects.

"Oh – a soft booty," Whispering, the barber continues his rant.

Boisterous laughter fills every chair.

Lincoln laughs a bit, but quickly his mind finds its way back to Alannah. Just as fast as the laughter came, it left as these thoughts arrived.

Shortly afterwards, Lincoln is waved over by his barber.

"LINC-LINC! What's good, sir? You alright?" his barber says after Lincoln sits down in the chair.

"Yeah, bro. All good. Everything's lovely. How's business?"

Snapping the barber cape, he drapes it across Lincoln's chest and legs. His barber replies, "They still trying to take the shop; but we won't let it happen. Talkin' bout this place isn't truly a landmark."

"STILL?! Even with all the things in place to protect it?"

"Yep. Big business don't care. Money is money and this place stands out like a sore thumb. They want all this area to look the same. Just boring-ass, tall gray buildings . . . with no soul."

"No soul is right!" another barber across from the two interjects.

"Damn," Lincoln looks at himself in the mirror.

Lincoln's barber places a device on his head, pressing a button that has the phrase 'Line Up' stamped on it. The device moves around Lincoln's forehead and ears, the sides, and back of his head. Then, his barber removes the device. A subtle light line resembling a chalk outline is around Lincoln's hairline. His barber uses this line to create a precision haircut.

During the haircut, the two talk more about a few things. Once his barber finishes, Lincoln pays for the cut and leaves.

He stops and looks around outside the shop, admiring the building and the fight the shop staff was committed to. Noticing a pretty woman walking towards him, Lincoln finds himself staring at the woman more than he should be.

Smiling back, the woman gives all the signs to welcome Lincoln over. For a moment, he wants to approach her.

What is going on with me? He thinks.

Chapter 9

STILL WATCHING THE WOMAN WALK AWAY, LINCOLN's phone buzzes. It snaps him out of his gaze, causing him to aggressively walk toward where his car was parked. As he sits inside his car, Lincoln clicks through the notifications on his phone. The buzz was a text message from Jake.

Hey, bud. Where ya at? Let's partake in some libation.

Lincoln stares out the window. *A drink wouldn't hurt*, he thinks. He promptly replies to the text.

Leaving the shop. Where y'all drinking at?

Showca$e. Jake replies.

SHOWCA$E?! IN THE MIDDLE OF THE DAY?!

DON'T JUDGE ME!

Showca$e was a private, VIP lounge that featured exclusive rooms used for strip and peep shows. Other rooms were used for much, much more. Patrons enjoyed this venue since it required a membership and reservations. Cell phones were not allowed beyond the lounge into the private rooms. Each patron was assigned a locker and key to store their phone.

Driving to the venue, Lincoln stops at a light. There he was met by a commuter bus to his left. An advertisement for a SINC could be seen on the side of the bus. The ad featured only a large, digital eye with several smaller pictures within the eye. The pictures were of various things, all involving a couple doing different activities. Near the eye is a phrase: EXPERIENCE SINCHRONY.

After arriving at Showca$e, Lincoln parked in a required designated valet area. He told the security at the door his name, which Jake had placed on a list. As a VIP, Jake could bring in two non-VIP people with him at any time. Though, he can only do this once a month and they must meet a drink minimum in the lounge.

Inside, Lincoln scans the large, dark room. He finally sees the back of Jake's head and Zeke to his side. "Yo! What's good? Where is Tommy?"

"Tommy couldn't make it. Last minute thing," Zeke says.

Jake takes a sip of something on the rocks. "Blessed be the man who created such a tasty beverage."

Without warning, Lincoln changes the subject awkwardly. "Hey, what y'all think about those robot things?

Zeke's eyebrows raise. "Robot things?"

"Yeah."

"There is artificial intelligence all over the place now. Be more specific," Zeke replies.

"Those, umm – "

"He's talking about SINCs, Zeke," Jake says, taking another sip. He stirs his glass gently, looking at the contents move about the glass.

"What about them?" Zeke leans forward, inquisitively.

A waitress comes over, interrupting the conversation.

"Anything I can get you gentlemen? More drinks? Or would you like to move to a private room? We have quite a few new girls."

"In a few, baby. Not yet. But please get my man here a whiskey," Jake says. The waitress nods and walks away. Jake cocks his head to the side. "The Lord is good."

Zeke sits back, crossing his legs. "What about them, Linc? You thinking about getting one?"

"LINC WITH A SINC!" Jakes says, laughing.

Zeke almost spits out his drink with laughter.

"Idiots." Lincoln looks around the room, doing his best to keep the conversation private. "Nah, nah, nah. Just wanted to know y'all thoughts about them."

"I don't see anything wrong with 'em. Those are the robots you can create, right? You can build your 'ideal woman,'" Zeke uses his fingers to make air quotes. "Shit. Go for it. What's the difference between us coming here and paying to see specific women dance?"

"They're not robots, though," Lincoln shakes his head.

"There is nothing more powerful than the natural warmth that God put into a woman's bosom. You won't find that with those things, Linc. Nothing but cold and emptiness," Jake says. "Go home to and enjoy your woman later. Enjoy that realness that the world seems to lack so much of."

Lincoln sighs. "Please. Don't mention Alannah in this conversation."

"Well, isn't that the reason for your question?" Zeke interjects.

Sighing, Lincoln leans back in his chair. "Relationships take work. I wouldn't do that – get one of those things. I was just curious."

After the waitress returns and gives Lincoln his drink, the three move into a private peep show room and talk more. While they talk and watch various flavors of women perform through the glass, Lincoln drinks and drinks more. Growing intoxicated, Lincoln begins to get angry as thoughts of Alannah grow in his mind. For some reason the women behind the glass remind him of her. At times, he even visualizes her face on their bodies.

Leaving the room abruptly, Lincoln grabs his phone from the security locker and sits at the bar. Opening his phone, he notices a missed text from Alannah.

Hey.

Lincoln is unsure on what to do. Alannah was the one who needed space and became hard to reach. *Why should I respond so quickly?* he thinks.

Lincoln doesn't respond. Instead, he spun the phone on the bar counter as he looked up at a television. Another ad for a SINC aired; one of the same ones he had seen before.

When Lincoln didn't respond in a timely fashion, Alannah calls him. Lincoln watches the phone ringing and still debates on answering. "When you coming home?" He says after finally picking it up, rather than providing a greeting first.

"Well, hey to you, too. Damn," Alannah says. "Wait. Are you drinking? You sound drunk."

Growing more irritated, Lincoln does his best to whisper. Still, he sounds aggressive. "Why are you not answering my question? When are you coming home?"

"You need to calm down and stop drinking, Lincoln. Where are you?"

"I'm out . . . getting SPACE!"

"Another round, sir?" the bartender at the lounge interrupts.

Lincoln nods, holding up his empty glass.

Sighing, Alannah pauses. "You know what – alright. Fine, Lincoln. I don't know when I'll coming home. This conversation alone has shown we need more time. I just wanted to say hello to your mean ass!" She hangs up before Lincoln can respond.

Frustrated, Lincoln launches his glass across the bar. He consequently shatters a few bottles of top-shelf liquor and a nearby mirror. Security swarms him, while some other management personnel go to retrieve Jake and Zeke.

"Okay, my guy. Time for you to go," a bald, burley man with a thick beard says. He gently puts his hands on Lincoln's arm.

"Get your fuckin' hands off me!" Lincoln swings at the security wildly, hitting him across his upper chest near his neck. The swing and slight miss spins Lincoln around, causing him to fall backwards into the man. Security grabs him under their arms aggressively.

"WHOA! WHOA! LINC!" Zeke shouts, witnessing the display.

"Alright! Let's go, bruh!" the burly man says, grabbing Lincoln by the back of his neck.

"EASY WITH HIM! PLEASE! HE'S GOING THROUGH SOME SHIT!" Zeke scrambles to get between the security team to assist.

"Who is the VIP responsible for this guest?" another security officer says.

Jake hesitantly holds his hand up, clearing his throat. "Me."

Management steps in between the group. "Your membership is suspended for a month. And you owe us for the damages."

"GOT DAMMIT, LINC!" Jake shouts, frustrated.

"FUCK THEM! THE WOMEN HERE ARE UGLY ANYWAY!"

Awakening the next day, Lincoln's head is pounding. He struggles to get off the couch, replaying as much of the day before that he can remember. Walking like a zombie, he goes to the refrigerator. There, he scans a menu on the automated screen of the refrigerator door. After locating 'hangover remedy,' he makes the selection by pressing the button near it. Moments later, he finds himself drinking the remedy at the kitchen table.

Turning on the television, he scans through the channels looking for something to watch. Upon finding a show, he leaves it on the channel. But then, another SINC commercial comes on. The commercial grabs his attention like all the others. Quickly he traverses his thoughts about Alannah, their relationship and all the things he has heard about these robots.

Fuck it, he thinks.

He is technically separated, with no sign in sight on when he and Alannah would be getting back together. *If* they would be getting back together. Who knows what she has been getting into? And it's been a long time since . . .

Lincoln sighs while grabbing his laptop. He begins clicking around to find more information about the SINCs. He looks at various images at first. He comes across posts on social media, where people have posed with their SINC lovers. Then he stumbles across a few reviews.

"OMG! What a wonderful experience!" someone wrote.

"I never thought I would try it, but I am glad I did!" another shared.

"I get my chores done in half the time!"

"If nothing else, SINCs are a wonderful ear when you need one. After my husband of twenty-five years suddenly died, I didn't know what I would do. Thank you to the makers of SINCs!" another reviewer posted.

"O . . . M . . . G. I AM IN LOVE!"

Lincoln rubs his brow, at times anxiously tapping his finger on his forehead. Finally, he locates the company's information for the SINC manufacturer. He stares at the front page of the website as if he's hypnotized for a few minutes. Yet, he is still unsure on how to proceed.

Chapter 10

WHILE LINCOLN WAS WORKING THE NEXT DAY, ALANNAH thought it would be ideal to go home for more things she needed. She could do it, after all, without interacting with Lincoln. Another argument or fight was not on her agenda for today.

For some reason, Lincoln had been leaving the alarm off; probably forgetting to turn it on. Usually, it was Alannah who reminded him. Because of this, Alannah was uncertain when Lincoln would be home.

For Alannah, the housesitting gig was like being at the spa for an extended stay. Now that she has gotten past the initial nervousness of the house and its contents, she refused to let anyone – including Lincoln – disrupt her plans for peace.

While at their community's gate, Alannah noticed more activity than usual at the corner store. Several men were standing around, conversing and acting suspiciously. She hadn't seen any of the men before in any of her trips coming or going from the front gate. One of the men noticed her and often awkwardly stared. During this moment, it seemed as if the gate was taking forever to open.

Another man from the group also noticed Alannah. Tapping the first man on the arm, the other man says something to him. Then, they both start walking toward Alannah's car slowly. But oddly, the gate still won't open fast enough. With all that Alannah has heard about the break-ins, she begins to panic.

Breathing heavily, Alannah tries scanning her hand again. And then again. At this point, she isn't giving the gate another chance to operate but still freaking out. Panicking more, she quickly puts up her window just as the men approach her car. One man taps on the glass, at which she yelps.

"Got any spare change, miss? We tryna get some sandwiches," one of the men says, as the other leans in beside him.

A light on the gate security reader changes, causing the gate to finally open. Alannah slams on the pedal, causing her tires to spin and squeal. She barely misses the gate, driving through it before it fully opens.

"WE JUST WANTED FOOD! BITCH!" one of the men yells, waving at the car in a frustrated fashion.

Speeding home, Alannah almost crashes the loaner car into a curb and a retaining wall. She parks erratically and runs into their home's garage. Then, she rushes into the kitchen. Grabbing some water, she chugs down the small bottle of filtered goodness as she continues to calm down. As she looks out of the window, Alannah wants to ensure that no one was following her. She notices that the yard was finally mowed and manicured.

Breathing better, Alannah looks over the house as if she didn't live there and was just visiting. She notices the empty hangover remedy bottle in the trash. Shaking her head, she continues to walk around. The house was a mess. Carry-out boxes and cups were everywhere. In their upstairs bedroom, Lincoln's clothes were scattered between the bed and a chair in the corner of the room that was supposed to be for relaxing. Instead, it was a mountain of laundry. It was as if Lincoln had given up while she had been gone.

But Alannah still missed him. She missed being home. She gently kneels by his side of the bed, burying her face into his pillow. She could still smell his scent. Getting into the bed, she noticed one of his tank tops at the edge of the bed. Grabbing it, she smelt it. Touching herself, she breathed heavily and quietly moaned. It's been a while since she has had this feeling.

Just as she was about to climax, birds who were having fun outside in the trees bang up against the bedroom window and startle her.

"Shit," she says aloud, staring at the ceiling like a kid who didn't want to get out of bed.

Alannah scans the rest of the room and the bathroom before going back downstairs. She feels better about her and Lincoln. Because she missed him and was able to have a special moment, Alannah knew that she still desired him. These feelings motivated her to clean up the home. So, she restocked the refrigerator with Lincoln's favorite foods and liquor.

Moving around with a tad bit of glee, Alannah's renewed happiness and pleasantries were quick lived. She suddenly noticed some strange, handwritten notes at the kitchen table. Lincoln's handwriting, clearly. After reading the notes, she does a web search on her phone and clicks through the findings. Only then did she realize that the notes were regarding SINCs.

"VIDA," Alannah says aloud.

"Hello, Alannah. What can I help you with?"

"What is SNAI Technologies?" Alannah asks, after skimming through the information on the computer screen.

"SNAI stands for Scientific Neuro-robotic Artificial Innovation. SNAI Technologies is a company founded by William E. Hildebrand in 2020. They specialize in the manufacturing of various types of neuro-robotics and devices that improve and advance the human brain. The company's most profitable and popular product is S.I.N.C. technology."

"VIDA, what does S.I.N.C. stand for?"

"S.I.N.C. stands for Sexually Intelligent Neuro-Robotic Companions."

Stunned, Alannah drops her phone. At first, she is appalled; angry and wants to call Lincoln to argue. But she quickly changes her mind after realizing that Lincoln wasn't really trying to improve things with her; that is, if he was researching a SINC. Instead, she takes pictures of his notes. Suddenly she becomes interested in the idea of a SINC for herself. She quickly reflects on how she felt when she saw the SINC in person at the house in the Hills, and how her curiosity grew substantially.

Alannah wasn't into playing games. *But maybe they both needed to experience some things. So that they could figure out if they felt strongly enough about each other. Did they truly want a future together or not?* she wonders.

Storming out of the house, she gets into the loaner car. Alannah backs up so fast that she almost hits one of her elderly neighbors.

"OH MY GOD! I'M SO SORRY!" Alannah shouts, after pressing the button to lower the window.

Walking around to the driver side of the car, the woman says, "You okay, child?"

"A lot on my mind, but yes. I'm okay. I'm sorry, truly."

Clearing her throat, the old woman pats Alannah on the arm. "It's okay. You shouldn't be driving if you can't focus on the road and what's around you. That's why they built those self-driving, thingamajigs." The woman points up toward the tall driving lanes in the mixing bowl above the city.

"Yes, I know. I'm sorry. I will be more careful." Alannah says.

"Did you hear about the break-ins?"

Alannah quickly remembers several minutes ago when she might have met the burglars. "I did."

"Please be careful, you hear?"

"I will. I promise." Alannah says. *Why does Lincoln keep leaving the alarm off? Now is not a good time to do that,* she thinks.

While he's working, Lincoln vents to his coworkers about his recent relationship frustrations over lunch. Most days he would buy lunch at a food truck a few streets over and eat at a table nearby. But today he needed company and didn't have the time.

Unbeknownst to Lincoln, he is being watched by the pretty assistant while he vents. It's obvious to some that she has a little bit more than a crush on him. The assistant listens to as much as she can hear from the distance. It's clear that Lincoln's relationship only hangs on by a thread.

As she listens, the assistant texts one of her friends.

Girl, guess what?

What? The friend replies.

Remember that guy I told you about? At work? His girl left him.

Oh no! The friend exclaims.

Yeah, girl. The assistant attaches a picture to the message, implying she is secretly planning something.

Don't be messy.

How is it messy? She left him! And now he is available!

While she continues texting, the assistant watches Lincoln gather up the trash from his lunch. Once he is alone, she quickly jogs over to him. She pretends to throw something away herself.

"Heyyy, Lincoln!"

Looking over his shoulder, Lincoln smiles a bit. "Hey! What's going on?"

"Nothing. I'm just finishing lunch. How are you?"

Lincoln isn't sure how to respond to that question. In the moment, he truly feels like shit. "Uh, I'm – I'm good. How are you?"

"Goood. Hey, you wanna get lunch tomorrow? My treat."

Lincoln stares at the pretty assistant, wondering on how to respond. He quickly follows the lines of her curves and inhales her scent. A chill goes down his spine.

"Can I let you know tomorrow?"

"Sure."

After work, Lincoln sits in his car and stares at the toll-free number he retrieved from the SINC's website. He thinks about Alannah and their problems. He further ponders his drunken behavior. Then he thinks about the assistant at work. *Messing around with her could get ugly. How cool would it be to have a non-emotional robot - that won't blow up my spot at work – to be at my beckon call*, he thinks.

Back in the Hills, Alannah has returned to housesitting. During the drive home, she had conflicted feelings after finding the notes Lincoln had left out. Suddenly she finds herself thinking about a lot of things, including the manager at the grocery store. *Would it be wrong just to have a drink with him? A little harmless conversation?* She thinks.

Upon arriving back at the house, she finds herself staring at the SINC woman in the glass again. Alannah wonders what the owner does with it. *How long did it take to create her? Why did the owner want her? Does he have sex with this thing? Is it really sex, if the other participant is not real?* She thinks.

The sun setting prompts certain lights to come on around the house. Various blinds are programmed to close at a certain time, causing other lights in the house to activate. When the nosy neighbor notices the house's lights coming on, he stops by. He rings the front doorbell, prompting a camera just above the door to begin recording.

"Yes?" Alannah says, standing near the security console.

"Hey there! Just wanted to check to see how things were going. Do you need anything? Can I come in?"

"No, I'm fine. How are you getting through the gate?" Alannah replies, hesitantly.

"Oh! I'm so sorry! I failed to mention that I have access. I am one of the emergency contacts for the owner since I live right down the hill. Listen, I'm sorry for startling you the other day. Let me know if you need anything."

Puzzled by the information, Alannah replies awkwardly. "Will do."

Chapter 11

LINCOLN CALLS SNAI TECHNOLOGIES DURING HIS RIDE home from work, so that he could learn more about the creation and manufacturing of the SINCs. The representative with whom he spoke didn't provide much information over the phone. Something about proprietary this and exclusive, sensitive information that. So, he scheduled an in-person orientation which would provide more details about the artificially intelligent robots. To his surprise, Lincoln could come in the next day.

Lincoln calls and informs his team lead at work that he had an emergency. He used this time off to drive about forty minutes south, where the orientation was located. The location was practically in the middle of nowhere.

Sitting in front of a tall, sophisticatedly designed building, Lincoln sat waiting in his car. The building had no name imprinted on it and no numbers marked its address. No logos or advertisements. It was oddly shaped, as if someone couldn't make up their mind whether the building should be a rectangle or an oval in some corners. All the windows were tinted. Only a few cars were scattered about in the parking lot, as if they weren't supposed to be there.

Lincoln stares at the building's surroundings and its entrance momentarily, working up the nerve to enter. Clearing his throat, he grabs his wallet and leaves his car.

Walking into the lobby, he encounters building security, who stop him almost immediately. Security personnel were positioned at desks and doors in three separate areas. Other staff had their own exclusive entrance and exit. Incoming visitors went one way, while outgoing visitors went another. There was only one way in and one way out for visitors.

After security checked in and scanned Lincoln twice, he was pointed toward the new client floor and given a special token device that only worked for the assigned floor. He was further instructed to always keep the device in his hand instead of his pocket. As he walked toward the nearby elevators, one opened immediately. It sensed his presence because of the device's sensor.

Lincoln's nervousness grows while he watches the numbers change on the digital screen at the top of the doors. He taps his leg with his fingers and can't seem to stand in one place. While deep in his thoughts, the elevator startles him upon arriving at the chosen floor. The elevator dings, causing the doors to open into a waiting room.

The environment feels cold and industrial, with completely white walls and loveseats positioned around it. It resembles the beginning stages of many buildings of which Lincoln oversaw the construction.

Lincoln is greeted by a slender, older woman sitting behind a desk. To her left and right are doors; one for entering and the other for exiting. Directly behind her is mirrored glass, where Lincoln notices his reflection. Other than him and the woman, the waiting room is completely empty.

"Hello. Mr. Dobson, is it? Lincoln Dobson?"

Lincoln clears his throat, hesitant to respond. "Uh, yes. I'm Mr. Dobson."

"Welcome! Please take this tablet and have a seat. Follow the automated menu to complete the questionnaire. When you are finished, click 'done.' Bring me back the tablet when your name is called."

Lincoln nods. He takes the tablet, sitting down awkwardly on one of the loveseats. At first the questionnaire was straightforward and asked him common questions.

Questions such as his gender, race, height and weight. His favorite food, color and hobbies. Where he was from and where he was currently located. Whether he was an only child or had siblings. Were his parents alive or dead? If alive, were they still together, separated or divorced?

The next set of questions were more intrusive. These questions related to sex, and the person's preferences. Questions such as what his sexual orientation was. Was he born a male? Did he like women, men or both? Had he ever experimented? Did he masturbate? If yes, how often and for how long? Was he a breast man or a butt man?

"Do I really need to answer all of these?" Lincoln awkwardly lifts his head, to see the woman behind the desk. He can feel his heart rate increase due to his anxiousness.

The older woman peeks over the desk. "I recommend you do so . . . and honestly . . . if you want the best experience possible with our technology. Your responses are confidential and will only be shared with your assigned doctor and appropriate staff."

A bit uncomfortable, Lincoln crosses his legs and sits back in the chair. He grows a little flush and sweats. He answers all the questions as honest as he could, without feeling embarrassed. But for some reason, it felt as if he was standing naked in front of a thousand people.

A short moment later, one of the doors click open. Someone walks out with a big smile on her face.

"Thank you, doctor! I can't wait!" she says to a person wearing a white lab coat.

"See you soon," the doctor replies. "Please continue toward that door."

Another employee walks with the woman to the door, ensuring she leaves through the correct exit.

Lincoln watches the exchange and begins feeling a bit better.

A few moments later, the opposite door opens. An attractive, young woman sticks her head out enough to be seen.

"Mr. Dobson?"

Raising his hand nervously, Lincoln nods and stands.

"Follow me, please."

Lincoln follows her closely, as she leads him down various glassed hallways. Most of the glass is frosted for privacy. But he can see the formations of people moving around the rooms. Unable to control his gaze, he watches the young woman from behind. Her hips and legs captivate him, even as they were hidden behind a lab coat.

"Please. Have a seat in here. Someone will be with you shortly," the woman says.

Lincoln nods nervously.

Another young, attractive woman comes into the room around five minutes later. "Would you like anything to drink, Mr. Dobson? Water? Coffee? Tea?"

Lincoln stammers. "Uh, no. Thanks."

The woman nods and then leaves.

Damn, all these fine women! Lincoln thinks.

Seconds later, a tall and average-built man walks into the room. His curly and faded hair is graying on the sides. He wears a similar lab coat, but it appears to be a different color from everyone else's. In his hand is a tablet and a cell phone.

"Mr. Dobson! Welcome! I am Dr. Glimmons. How are you?"

"Hey. A bit nervous, but good."

The doctor sits down in a plush office chair across from Lincoln. He adjusts his necktie so that it is not in his way. "I can tell. Most who come in for these orientations are nervous."

Lincoln nods.

"But you have liked what you have seen thus far, hmm?"

"Who? Your office ladies?"

The doctor nods gleefully. "Yes. Based on your readings, you grew excited upon seeing them. No?"

"Uh, um..."

"The device you are holding not only controls the elevator. It also monitors your heart rate and much more!"

Lincoln opens his sweaty palm, staring at the device. "Damn. I forgot I was holding this thing."

"Yes, yes! Most people do. We have been studying you from the moment you checked in."

Lincoln's eyebrows raise; his eyes widen. He doesn't know what to say.

"I will take the device. Tell me what brings you in today." The doctor turns his chair and crosses his legs, activating his tablet. He reaches out for the device at which Lincoln was still gazing.

"Honestly, I'm not sure." Lincoln says, sliding forward in his seat to hand the doctor the device.

"That's okay. Plenty of our clients aren't usually certain. Through our comprehensive process, though, we can help them decide if our technology is right for them. This device starts that process."

Lincoln leans back in his chair, relaxing.

"Do you believe you want more sexual attention? Emotional attention? Or just plain ole company? Or *all that and then some*, like my momma used to say."

Lincoln chuckles a little, looking around the room. He doesn't know how to respond, because he doesn't know why he is at this orientation in the first place.

"Let's try a different route. How about I tell you a bit about the company and the process? Then we'll go from there."

Nodding, Lincoln replies, "That – that sounds good."

"Well, as I stated, I am Dr. Phil Glimmons. I am one of over fifty doctors that work for SNAI Technologies. We have three locations within a sixty-mile radius. Here, Marlay and Covington. The company was founded in 2015 but changed its name. It went public in 2020 by William E. Hildebrand. Hildebrand was a doctor in neuroscience and robotics. He spent about twenty years experimenting with various technology. As time went on, he made several, ground-breaking advancements. Later he decided to branch off and started this company. Plainly put, he is a *genius* . . . who found a way to combine robotics with the human brain.

"Most people come in because they are interested in exploring a lifestyle with our SINCs. SINC is an acronym, which stands for Sexually Intelligent Neuro-Robotic Companions. In laymen's terms, our SINCs are artificially created robots that are programmed with tons and tons of data to perform as if they were human. Perform as in being able to speak and respond to commands and walk and move as if they are human. All these features are inside of a body that looks like you want them to. And they don't get old; they don't die."

Lincoln's eyebrows raise. "Shit."

The doctor laughs and continues. "Shit is right. Our clients vary from the extremely wealthy, to all the way down to the average Joe. Like the questions I asked you, we have asked others. Some of our clients have wanted specific things from our SINCs. A unique experience if you will. Others just wanted some sort of emotional support. But most of our clients want an out of this world sexual experience that they can't seem to find on their own. Still with me?"

Lincoln clears his throat, nodding.

"I know this is a lot of information. Stop me if you have any questions."

"No, no. I'm good. No questions yet."

"Okay. Each doctor like myself has a role. Depending on what your needs are, we have doctors that analyze your behavior first." The doctor quickly types something into his tablet as he talks, after looking at the small device that he took from Lincoln.

"My behavior?" Lincoln leans forward, resting his arms on his legs.

"Yes. Things you like, don't like. Sexual things. Physical things. Emotional things like that which angers you. What makes you happy? What traumas have you experienced? Fight or flight, etc. My role is to do a general assessment before moving you further along in the process."

Lincoln looks away. "Man. That sounds like a long time."

"Yes. We operate a very thorough ship with our products. Are you looking for something more short term?" The doctor leans forward and rests his arms on his desk.

"Do you have that option?"

"Well, let me back up first. I'm getting a little ahead of myself, because I want you to have the best experience possible. But . . . a little more explanation." The doctor grabs a remote on his desk, points it at an adjacent wall and clicks a button. A digital presentation appears, displaying the information he has been sharing with Lincoln verbally. "We design our SINCs by combining large amounts of data that we get from behavioral studies of various types of people. We combine this data with a specific behavior study of the person who would be interacting with the SINC - which would be you in this case. We use fast, iterative processing and intelligent algorithms, allowing the software to learn automatically from certain patterns or features in the data. At the core of the SINC is a neural network made up of interconnected units like the neurons in our human bodies. It processes information by responding to external inputs, relaying information between each unit. We have several different neural networks that can be inserted into your companion and updated to your liking. Basically, it's like updating or reinstalling a computer you already own. We can program our product to adjust to your desires."

"Meaning?"

"Meaning, we program your SINC to react to your voice and commands, body language, scents, impulses and neurological centers. So, it's as simple as a thought or verbal instruction. Your wish is the SINC's command. But this is the long-term approach. This approach takes weeks and sometimes months to complete. But we also have a more, short-term approach that is less involved."

"And what comes with that?" Lincoln asks.

"Essentially, we give you the best, pre-owned SINC that we have available, based on what you tell us that you want and the basic information that you provided us. Moreover, it's based on the information we were able to collect from this device." The doctor holds the device up and wiggles it.

Lincoln chuckles, "So . . . y'all would give me someone else's toy that has been used and abused?"

"No, not quite," the doctor smiles. "We adjust the programming and sanitize the device thoroughly. It goes through several rounds of quality checks. Then, it's looked over one last time by our analysts and doctors. Once the SINC goes through several rounds of approvals, it becomes available. You would never know someone else owned it. It would look and feel brand-new."

Lincoln becomes quiet as his thoughts move rapidly. His reservations cause him to doubt the process. Being a private person, sharing so much about himself makes him uncomfortable. What's more was that this idea was starting to sound expensive. Even the short-term approach seemed too much.

Pacing in front of the presentation, the doctor continues. "This option is actually pretty popular by those who are in a certain financial bracket and those who aren't too . . . sure on what they want."

"Hmm."

"Would you like a tour? I can show you some areas of our facility."

"That would be dope," Lincoln replies.

"And dope it is. Follow me."

The doctor leads Lincoln down a few hallways to another set of private elevators that only the personnel use. For the doors to open, a successful PIN and biometric reading entry must occur. Once they are on another floor, the doctor shows Lincoln the room where several analysts and programmers sit. Each of these people sit at various desks, some with three or more monitors in front of them. Sounds of keys clicking and various machinery rings throughout the room.

In another area, technicians are building the core elements to the SINCs. Wires, processors, batteries and hydraulics and more are scattered around. Across from the room, more technicians are building the robots' exterior elements. Heads, arms, torsos and legs. Breasts, vaginas, penises and other uniquely designed body parts.

"Oh shit," Lincoln says, in awe.

"Yeah. Some of our client's want a *distinctive* . . . experience."

"But they . . . why . . . how do they look so real? Like – like they're human? They really look human!"

The doctor smiles but says nothing.

A technician paints the nails of an almost completed female SINC. An artist designs a tattoo on a fully completed specimen. Another technician speaks into a device, testing the response of the SINC. Another employee detaches a face from the rest of the head of a SINC, flipping it over to review the wires attached to it from the other side.

While in amazement of the behind the scenes of this place, Lincoln fails to notice a woman employee. She had already walked by him and the doctor twice. She had been eyeing Lincoln intensely. The third time she comes by, he finally sees her and the two lock eyes. Her stare was eerie but intriguing. Intriguing enough that Lincoln tries to get closer to her without leaving the doctor's side, but before he can, the woman goes into a restricted room.

"Well, that ends the tour. Here, take my card. When you are ready, contact us," the doctor says.

Lincoln nods. "Will do. Thanks."

As Lincoln later leaves the orientation, he is perplexed by the woman's gaze. He thinks about this more while sitting at a light just a block away from the orientation location.

Several miles away, Alannah is at the grocery store not far from her and Lincoln's home. She made up an excuse to go to the store again, subconsciously hoping to run into the grocery store manager, Exton. Wearing large sunglasses, she hopes to not be seen by anyone she knows. Once she arrives at the store, she pretends to be browsing while keeping an eye out for him. He doesn't seem to be there.

"Can I help you with something, miss?" a voice says from behind her. The voice was different than what she had been hoping.

When she turns around, the manager on duty was not the person she had been expecting. Instead, it was a young kid with glasses and excessive acne. An overachieving kid that made it to management early in his life perhaps.

Feeling a bit ashamed, Alannah says, "Um, no. I think I am good. But, um, you aren't the same manager that was here the other day?"

"Oh, no. I'm not, sorry. You must be talking about Exton. Regional management has him at another store for the next few days. Is there something I can help you with? Do I need to relay a message to him?"

"No, no. Thanks." Alannah looks around embarrassingly, before briskly leaving the store.

Chapter 12

GOING TO WORK THE NEXT DAY, LINCOLN REVIEWS his bank statement while driving. Does he have the funds for a pre-owned SINC? Shaking his head, he feels like such an idiot having gone to that orientation. Embarrassment covers his body like summer heat. *Why spend money on something like that? Especially when ole girl at work is willing to give it to me for free? AND SHE'S HUMAN*, he thinks. Plus, money is tight with Alannah being technically unemployed. His conflictions cause him to renege on his initial thoughts regarding the SINC.

Just as he walks into one of the trailers at his job, Lincoln is bombarded by a couple of his team members. "What up, Linc?! You won't believe what we heard this morning!"

"What?"

"Please tell me you didn't go get one of those robot-things you were talking about the other day!"

I gotta stop running my mouth, Lincoln thinks. "Shh, shh. Man. Keep y'all voices down," he says, looking around. "Nah. I didn't. Why?"

"The owner of that company is a racist! Look at this!" a team member replies, handing Lincoln his phone.

On the phone is an article his team member had been reading. It stated how the founder of SINCs was one of many wealthy white people who supported and funded racially charged events in the past. Hildebrand contributed to many fundraising efforts that had been organized by racist and prejudice organizations.

Hildebrand was further quoted to have been a member of various anti-equality groups, stating that 'whites were the superior race.' Also stating that 'all lives mattered.' The article goes on, stating that the SINCs were initially designed for only 'a certain class of people.' Moreover, it suspected that a law-enforcement and security version of the SINC technology was in the works. This new version would soon be released under a different name, to mostly 'troubled communities.'

"Get the fuck outta here," Lincoln mouths quietly.

"You see that?! What the hell is a 'certain class of people' and 'troubled communities'?"

The first team member chimes in, "That company is racist, Linc."

Walking away from the group, Lincoln feels like a child that has been scolded. So, he goes into his office and sits down. A few hours pass as he catches up on some work. He had been making good progress until his father called him.

Because he has a special ringtone selected for his dad, Lincoln doesn't look at it when it rings. 'Superstition,' by Stevie Wonder. A classic, soul melody that his pop enjoyed. "Hey, dad. What's up?"

"DID YOU SEE THAT SHIT?!" his father practically screams into the phone.

"See what?"

"That story about that racist owner of those robots?"

Lincoln reclines in his chair, shaking his head. "Are you and my coworkers talkin' or something?"

"What do you mean?" his father replies.

"Nothing. Yeah, I saw it," Lincoln replies, moving some papers around on his desk.

"Can you believe what that man said?"

Getting up, Lincoln closes his office door. "You of all people shouldn't be surprised. You were out there protesting AGAINST people like him back in the day."

"I was! Twenty, thirty-something years later we are still dealing with the same shit! Repeatedly."

"But you taught me that these types of people will never change. They will just continue to infect others. The cycle continues."

"You can't make anyone change. They must . . . WANT to change. All we can do is make our voices heard and lead by example. Continue to fight for what's ours."

"True."

"Now you see why we fought so hard to keep the shop!"

Lincoln sighs. "Yeah, I know. But I gotta go, dad. I will come see you later. I gotta work."

"Okay."

Hanging up the phone, Lincoln slowly becomes infuriated at himself. His relationship was not well. He had been drinking more than usual, and almost catching a beat-down because of it. Now, he was about to buy a silly product from a racist company. His father would be ashamed of him.

Looking out the window to collect his thoughts, Lincoln notices the pretty assistant walking toward his trailer. He almost forgot that he promised to let her know about lunch. Scrambling, Lincoln bolts out a side door. He runs in the opposite direction before he could be seen.

After work, Lincoln heads to his father's home. It's about thirty minutes northwest of where he lives with Alannah. His father still lives in the same middle-class area in which Lincoln was raised. These properties have substantially gone up in value after many years; though, most of this area has not been gentrified because of opposition from the people living there. Residents banded together. They worked with various churches, businesses and politicians to keep big corporations from leveling their historic homes.

The process took many years. But despite their efforts, these corporations continued their threats.

Lincoln parks in his father's driveway and goes to the mailbox, where he retrieves his father's mail. His father still likes to receive physical mail, refusing to go digital and paperless. Afterwards, Lincoln walks to the door, pushes it open and walks in without a key.

"Dad, it's me."

"I know. I saw you on this," His father holds up his tablet. An alert on the tablet showed a brief video of activity occurring within his front yard. "Check it out."

A short clip plays. It shows Lincoln arriving in his car, checking the mail and walking toward the front door.

"When did you get that?"

"The other day," his father proudly responds.

"And here I thought you were against a bunch of technology."

"I am. But those white-collar assholes keep coming by here. They are threatening us with lawsuits if we don't sell.

Like we haven't already been to court a thousand times already. And those house-to-house salespeople. And those pushy religious folk. With this, I can see them all coming."

"And do what once you see them?"

Lincoln's father holds up his hybrid, snub-nosed, double-barreled shotgun that was positioned just by his chair. It was a cross between a miniature shotgun and a handgun.

"Dad, why did you buy that? That gun hasn't had enough testing yet. I heard the recoil is crazy on that thing."

"I tested it. I can handle it," his father says, looking at it closely.

"Tested it where?"

"Don't worry about all that, son."

Lincoln scoffs, "And you can't go pulling a gun on old ladies that come to talk about Jesus. You can't pull a gun on anyone. You will go to jail, Pop! Self-defense is the only option."

"No, no, no boy. The gun is for the white-collar assholes. I just scream profanities through this app at the old Bible ladies. They get offended and leave."

Lincoln shakes his head.

"I still don't believe in too much technology. We have become reliant on a bunch of useless shit. Nobody uses maps anymore. Nobody cleans their own homes or gardens – nothing! LAZY!"

"No doubt about that," Lincoln looks through a stack of papers on his father's table nearby.

"How in the hell can we spend so much time, money and energy on these things – self-driving cars, robots and shit – and we still got the homeless in the streets? And black folk who still need reparations!"

Lincoln nods in agreement.

"Anyway. How are you and the misses?"

Looking away, Lincoln clears his throat depressingly. He shrugs.

"That bad, huh?"

"We fight almost every day over the smallest stuff."

"You know what's going on when y'all do that, don't you?"

Lincoln shrugs again, as if he doesn't care about the subject.

His father continues, not expecting a response. "Y'all forgot how to communicate. And this is your new normal. See . . . it's easy to communicate in the beginning when things are fresh. Especially when most of the talking is in the bed, or when just your surface needs are being met. That new, fresh shit. You know what I'm talking about. But once you get to where you and Alannah are – a few years in – or shit, even just several months in for some people – it takes deeper communicating and understanding for the relationship to work. You need to sit down and ask each other plainly, 'What's wrong and what are some solutions to fixing it?' 'What are your expectations of me in this relationship, at this moment?' Talk about your spiritual and emotional needs."

Reclining back in his chair, Lincoln breathes heavily and crosses his arms. He looks away, holding back a tear or two.

"I don't think you have healed enough from the miscarriage. You might also be blaming Alannah for part of it. It's not her fault. It's not yours."

Lincoln bursts into tears, leaning forward onto his legs so that his face is covered.

His father gets up slowly. His knees not as good as they used to be. He kneels in front of Lincoln, putting both hands-on Lincoln's shoulders. "It's alright. It's alright. Let it out. Takes a strong man to cry and then get better. Any idiot can get angry and stay angry." As Lincoln gathers himself and calms down, his father stands up. "When you're finished, go get the mop. Cause I just cleaned my floors and you in here messing them up again."

Both laugh.

A few hours later, Lincoln tries to relax at the pool hall. He was going to go straight home once he left his father's place but decided to take a moment to clear his head. His father's words were heavy but uplifting at the same time. So, he stopped by and shot a few rounds alone, and got some drinks thereafter.

While at the pool hall, Lincoln doesn't realize that the woman employee from his SINC orientation was also there. She was sitting alone across the bar from Lincoln, dressed down and missing her glasses. Liquor bottles and televisions blocked their views from each other.

Finally noticing the woman, Lincoln scratches his head. He wondered where he had seen her before. She looked quite familiar to him. The woman noticed him as well, and almost at the same time.

"Hey, Lizzy!" Lincoln shouts to the bartender.

"Hey, you want another?"

"Not yet. But whatever she is drinking, send her another," Lincoln replies, nodding in the direction of the woman.

"Sure thing."

As the bartender pours the woman another drink, Lincoln watches as the woman questions the bartender on why another glass had been placed in front of her. Telling the woman something, the bartender points at Lincoln. Lincoln then gets up and begins to walk around the large bar toward where the woman sat. But before he could get to her, she aggressively pays and leaves the area before exiting out the front entrance.

"What happened?" Lincoln asks, turning toward the bartender.

The bartender shrugs. "Not sure." She looks at the most recent transactions on a computer screen. "But damn. I like the way she tips!"

After consuming a few more drinks, Lincoln leaves the pool hall tipsy. Despite his best judgement, he gets into his car and begins his route home. He speeds through a few traffic lights, but then, he notices that a car behind him seems to have been following him for a few miles.

Jumping from his car at the next red light, he leaves his door open and runs toward the car behind him. But just as he approaches the car, the person behind the wheel speeds off around him. Staring intentionally, he realizes it was the same woman from the pool hall. Quickly he gets out his phone and types the tag number into a text message, saving it as a draft.

Unbeknownst to him, the woman from the pool hall was also the employee from his orientation. She had been following him; although, Lincoln couldn't figure out why should would do this, regardless of who she was. Trying to gather his thoughts, Lincoln notices a card on the ground. He bends over, picks it up and flips it over. Lincoln sees that it is an advertisement for SINCs, but the eyes of one of the SINC women were crossed out with the letter X darkly. Below the picture, someone wrote the phrase: stay away.

Chapter 13

LYING IN BED WITHIN ONE OF THE LARGEST GUEST ROOMS, Alannah stares at the wall art as the blinds automatically open at sunrise. The sun pierces through the blinds, creating art of its own. It manipulates the light in the room, creating shadows in various places. For some reason, she hasn't slept well since she has been in this home. Getting comfortable was a challenge.

Turning on her side, Alannah reflects on everything she has been through over the past several days and weeks. She misses Lincoln something terrible but going home only gives him more power over her emotionally. She is quite aroused by the grocery store manager, but she has never contemplated cheating on any person she dated. Moreover, her relationship with Lincoln is by far the longest relationship she had ever been in.

When things didn't work in previous relationships, she would just walk away when her efforts didn't improve them. But she has been with Lincoln for a while now, and so she still has hope that things would work out. *What's wrong with a little fun? Especially if Lincoln is having some. I don't need to know what he is doing, and he doesn't need to know what I am doing*, she thinks.

Alannah was so absorbed in thoughts that she became startled when her phone buzzes on the nightstand. She clicks on it a few times and notices a text message from Sherrie.

Heyyyy, girl! Greetings from Colombia, South America! I'm about to hop on my next flight. But more importantly, I am texting you because the homeowner needs you for a few more days. You in? They are willing to pay you double the rate for the short notice.

Without hesitation, Alannah agrees.

Cool! I will let them know. And we need to go out when I get back. Been in the air non-stop it seems like. I haven't had a drink in days. I need to turn up on somebody's dance floor!

Turning over onto her back, Alannah stares at the ceiling. She wants to call Lincoln to say hello; though feels as if she has been doing most of the work in their relationship, including initiating communication. She further feels a bit selfish, because, *what if Lincoln hadn't been doing anything wrong? While she had been flirting and looking for a man she had no business talking to,* she thinks. *Yes, Lincoln had researched SINCs, but he was too cheap to get one, right? And he has never given me a reason to think he would cheat,* Alannah further ponders.

Clicking on her phone, Alannah decides to call him.

"Hey," Lincoln answers, groggily.

"Hey. I know I woke you."

Lincoln lets out a large yawn. "You alright?"

"Yeah. You?"

"Yeah."

"Okay," Alannah says, speaking in a tone that indicated she had more to say.

A silence fell over the conversation.

"Well, I need to get up in a few for work. Need to try to get a few more minutes of sleep." Lincoln says dryly.

"Okay. Have a good day. Bye."

"Bye."

Alannah sighs. She's somewhat stunned that Lincoln wasn't angry, or that he didn't press her with a bunch of questions. Getting up and walking to the bathroom, Alannah brushes her teeth and twirls her hair into a bun. She then walks toward the kitchen. She double backs to thinking about the SINC already in the home, finding herself staring at it in amazement.

Unable to go back to sleep, Lincoln stares at his phone. He replays the brief and awkward conversation he had with Alannah. As much as he hated to admit it, he missed his woman. He wanted her home but was done begging. Fortunately, he was too tired to question her.

He clicks through his phone and checks social media. An ad for a SINC randomly appears, annoying him. After closing social media, he brings up the draft text message. It still had the woman's license plate number in it. He tried to make sense of what happened but couldn't figure out why she would be stalking him.

Lincoln first showers and gets dressed for work. Then he calls Zeke for help. Who better to call than someone that does background investigations?

"Hello?"

"What up?!" Lincoln says anxiously.

Zeke groans like a hibernating bear that had been awoken early. "Damn, Linc. It's early. You good?"

"Sorry, man. Need your help."

Zeke yawns. "This must be important."

"Indeed."

"What's up?"

Lincoln explains everything, even admitting that he went to an orientation about SINCs. He further explains the stalking at the pool hall and what occurred on the road thereafter. After getting made fun of for a few minutes, he manages to persuade Zeke to research the license plate which he had managed to jot down. Zeke agrees to investigate it, telling him that he would speak to him later.

Before he leaves for work, Lincoln notices that the refrigerator was full. In fact, so was the liquor inventory. Various clothing had been put in the dirty clothes bin or washed, while the trash had been taken out. *Had Alannah been home? Or did she call that cleaning service that he hated again?* He thinks. Anytime the cleaning people came, they moved his stuff around. It seemed like he could never find anything.

Lincoln gets through most of the day as normal. Everything seemed to be going well at the site including flooring, electrical and lighting, painting and accessories, and the required inspections between. And so, he left work feeling a bit different. He couldn't pinpoint what the feeling was. Was he getting used to Alannah being gone? Was this what freedom felt like? He continued walking toward his car while traversing his thoughts, but then a voice shouts out at him.

"Hey, Lincoln!" the assistant says, excitedly.

Stopping in his tracks, Lincoln turned around slowly. *Shit*, he thinks. He realizes he failed again to stay clear of her. "Hey, Shelly. What's up?"

"I missed you the other day. Lunch?"

Quickly Lincoln ponders the idea of hanging out with Shelly. Technically he is separated in his relationship, and he has no intent on anything more than a harmless outing with a coworker. "Oh, damn. That's right. How about happy hour? Are you free now? If not, that's okay. I know its short notice--" Lincoln replies.

"Yes, yes! I am free," Shelly interjects excitedly.

Lincoln offers to drive. He and Shelly venture to a nearby Mexican bistro. Shelly orders a margarita while Lincoln orders a specialty cocktail on the happy hour menu. The outing starts off wonderfully until the liquor begins to sink into Lincoln more. The more he drank, the clearer it became that he was hurt by the state of his relationship with Alannah. Without realizing it, he had dominated the conversation he and Shelly were having. All the topics were something about Alannah.

"Wow, you really miss her, don't you?" Shelly eventually says dryly, looking at her watch a few times. She sits back and folds her arms, ready to leave at this point. Lincoln has become a charity case in her mind. "Is that her picture on your phone?"

A notification caused Lincoln's phone to illuminate. It displayed a digital wallpaper of Alannah from a recent outing.

"Oh, shit. My bad. I'm rambling, ain't I?" Lincoln puts his phone away. "Yeah, that's her."

Shelly doesn't say anything, raising her brows as if she agrees. "She's pretty."

"Thanks."

"You know, you should come out tonight. I'm going to Ritme Lounge. Me and some friends are going to hang out. Sounds like you need to get out, too."

Lincoln strokes his chin, contemplating the idea. "Oh yeah? Text me the place. I may check it out."

The conversation starts to improve, mostly because Shelly is ecstatic that Lincoln might come party with her after hours. Things quickly went from very awkward to normal again. After changing the subject and talking more, they wrapped things up. Lincoln took Shelly back to her car.

On his way home, Lincoln pulled up to a traffic light as it turned red. Lincoln noticed a homeless man, who had busted into traffic without a care, moving erratically in the streets near his car. Walking up and down the lanes, the man yells random things. He pointed at a large billboard advertisement for SINCs atop a building. He also held a similar ad in his hand, like the one the mystery woman dropped. The eyes of the SINCs were X'd out the same way.

Jumping in front of Lincoln's car, the homeless man says, "Oh, my sisters and brothers – please, please. Hear me when I say that the Lord didn't intend for us to use the gift of technology this way. The home and bed are a sacred place, meant only for human man and human woman to share. Neither robot and woman, nor robot and man. Vile, vile, vile! We serve a jealous God. He will strike down those that compete with him! As the good book says in Exodus 20:3-4 'Thou shalt have no other gods before me. Thou shalt not make unto thee any graven image, or any likeness of anything that is in heaven above, or that is in the earth beneath, or that is in the water under the earth.' Y'all ought to be ashamed of yourselves. Using these robots in this way. Stick to letting them vacuum your floors and tell you the time. Not this sick shit! We are doomed as a people!"

Horns blared. Meanwhile, the man blocked other vehicles while continuing to move about crazily. Eventually he returned to Lincoln's car, tapping on the glass of the driver-side window. He lifted and shook his cup aggressively. Lincoln opened the window, placing a couple dollars in it. Nodding, the man walked away and continued to speak his truth.

Later that evening, Alannah readied herself for a night out. She curled her hair and let her locks flow naturally over her shoulders. She then took time to figure out an outfit. Eventually, she put on a sleeveless V-neck, paired with a tie-around waist skirt. Since she had not been out in a while, Alannah needed this night of fun. She had been through a lot recently, especially with the state of her relationship. She only allowed herself a coffee date with her friends, or a quick happy hour after work. But a late night of drinking and dancing had been a long time coming. So, she began doing her hair and getting dressed. Then, she drove down from the house in the Hills to meet Sherrie at the Ritme Lounge.

The downtown Fellington lounge was located near the waterfront. Resident DJs provided sets of music most nights, but tonight a live cover band was scheduled in the main room.

After Alannah gave her car to an automated valet service, she got into a short line leading to the lounge's lobby. Since she got there before Sherrie and her other friends, she must wait. The lobby had multiple hallways, each leading to different rooms playing different music. The main dance area was designated for the cover band.

Sherrie, Monica and Elina arrive shortly after Alannah. All greet each other and provide the lounge staff with a special barcode that a promoter gave Sherrie. It gets them into the VIP area for free. Also, it gives each person their first two drinks for free.

Once inside, the four women talk and laugh amongst themselves. They scan and observe the room's climate. Excitedly, Elina pulls Alannah and Sherrie by their hands onto the dancefloor, Monica in tow. The four dance amongst themselves, smiling from ear to ear as they move to the sounds provided by the band. The melodies and rhythms moved throughout the room, vibrating every soul.

Elina disappears for a few minutes, returning with three drinks in her hands. But then, she awkwardly spills some of the drinks because of the crowded room. Returning to the bar, she rejoins the group with one of the bartenders, whom was helping her hold some of the drinks.

Alannah sips her martini, doing her best to dance without spilling it. After a few sips, a feeling comes over her; a high she hadn't felt in a while. Goosebumps covered her arms and her heart as she moved to the bass of the music. A warm tingling feeling seemed to travel all over her body. She felt alive for the first time in months; years maybe. The rush of the environment was intoxicating.

Watching the activity from above, Exton – the grocery store manager – leans on a railing and moves his head to the beat. He sips on a beer, with a couple of his friends to his side, as he cases the room like hunters looking for potential prey. As Exton's eyes follow the movements of the various women on the dance floor, he is stunned. He sees a familiar face dancing not far from the bar.

Moving briskly down the stairs, Exton turns his body to squeeze between the various people moving throughout the room. His eyes lock on Alannah, as if he was stuck in a weird dream and Alannah was a glowing light leading to the way out. Exton is practically hypnotized. He watches the way her body moves to the music, and how the lighting radiates her skin.

Coming up behind Alannah like a lion stalking wildebeest, Exton reaches out and gently touches her arm. As Alannah continues to dance, she turns around rhythmically to face whoever was touching her. Her mouth drops in awe upon recognizing Exton standing in front of her. Without saying a word, the two begin dancing closely. Their bodies practically connect at the seams of their outfits. Alannah's friends all raise an eyebrow at the sight in front of them.

After a blend of a few songs, Alannah decides to finally say something to Exton. "What are you doing here? Are you following me or something?"

"I should be asking you that!" Exton laughs, spinning her around.

Alannah pretends to be offended. "What are you talking about?"

Exton gets close enough to speak into Alannah's ear. "My co-worker told me that you came looking for me."

"Ah, shit." Alannah shakes her head. "I forgot about that. I shouldn't have done that. Sorry."

"Sorry? Why? I like a woman who isn't afraid to show a man she is genuinely interested."

Alannah smiles, raising her eyebrows. "Interested? Who said I'm interested?"

Exton's mouth can't seem to close. He's shocked by Alannah's response. He doesn't know what more to say at this point.

Alannah laughs.

Before he could respond, Alannah introduces him as a former co-worker to her friends. The group continues dancing in a small huddle, as if they created their own VIP section in the middle of the dance floor.

Moving closer to Alannah, Exton pulls her to him. He places his hands around her and puts them on her lower back. As they move to the melody, his hands begin sliding down Alannah's waist. Quickly Alannah pulls herself away, continuing to dance as if she didn't know what Exton was trying to do. Seconds later, Exton pulls her close again and stares into her eyes. Alannah slows down her dancing, as if she is under Exton's spell.

Leaning into her, Exton closes his eyes. He opens his mouth, reaching to place his lips on hers. Just as he gets close enough, Alannah turns her face. It causes him to awkwardly kiss her cheek at the corner of her mouth.

Shelly, the co-worker from Lincoln's job, is seen standing on an adjacent platform. She had been dancing and enjoying herself as well, patiently waiting on Lincoln to reply to her text message that she sent moments ago.

Sorry. I can't make it, Lincoln says.

With a disappointed expression, she sends him a sad face emoji. Seconds later, she notices Alannah. Shelly watches her for a while, envious of the woman who had something she wanted. She keeps a jealous eye on the woman who had captured Lincoln's heart. She was shocked when she saw Alannah in the venue. She was even more shocked upon noticing Alannah dancing so sensually with a man who was clearly not Lincoln. So, she pulled out her phone and took some pictures and a video of most the dance -- including what seemed to be a kiss. But from her vantage point, she couldn't tell for sure. The environment was dark. Regardless, she had the information she didn't know she needed. She hoped it would help her get the man she had a crush on for quite a while.

Chapter 14

SITTING ON THE HOME'S BACK DECK THE NEXT MORNING, Alannah relaxes by the large, woodland-style pool. She reflects on the night before. Alannah is still a bit aroused by the exchange between her and Exton; so much so that it's as if her body is throbbing and still within his embrace. It's been a while since she's felt an urge take her over in this way.

After responding to friends' texts about the mystery man, Alannah begins to feel guilty. Her friends hadn't believed that Exton was just an old co-worker. How did something so innocent become such a big deal? Was she willing to risk it all by publicly pursuing this behavior?

Once again, she contemplates the SINC idea. At least there could be some privacy if she were to go this route. She has bonus money from housesitting, so why not? *Is it cheating if the other person isn't a person at all? No different than a dildo, right? A walking, talking dildo,* Alannah thinks, laughing a little aloud to her own thoughts.

As much as she would love being in the company of a young, chiseled being like Exton, it would be wrong. Even if it started off harmless, she knew what path it would take. *With a SINC, I could just . . . talk to it, and not worry about it trying anything,* she thinks more.

Alannah talks herself into calling SNAI Technologies. She schedules an orientation for later in the evening to discuss more about the SINCs at the closest location to the Hills. Going south again was something she didn't want to do. She was a bit tired and hungover from partying. Besides, she didn't want to run into Lincoln or his friends. More importantly, she didn't want to be tempted with Exton. It seemed as if he was showing up more in her life, and she couldn't figure out why. Looking for him that one day didn't help.

She was surprised she could get in for the SINC orientation so soon. Calling from the home in the Hills seemed to have alerted the company that she was of a certain status. (She didn't want to use her cell phone.) At the time, someone else had cancelled their appointment. Her timing of the call was perfect.

A few hours later, Alannah drove forty minutes to the orientation. During the drive, Chase from work sent a text message to tell her that there had been no change to Alannah's duties. Further motivation for her to live her life and enjoy some downtime, because anything can happen.

Once at the SINC location, Alannah purposely walks inside and experiences similar security checks. She sits in a waiting room, unknowingly similar to what Lincoln had experienced during his orientation. Almost everything is the same. The building, the lobby and the waiting room designs are all identical.

She looks at the small device that she was given, placing it down on the table beside her. Then, she completes the questionnaire. Afterwards, she looks at various digital advertisements about the technology.

"Alannah Laghari," a woman wearing a lab coat pokes her head from behind a door and into the waiting room.

"Yes."

"Please follow me. And bring that with you," the woman says, pushing the door open wider. She points to the device that Alannah had put down.

Walking down a hallway, various attractive male employees walk by Alannah. The woman employee, being of different ethnicity, height and build, also walks by her – as do a few women.

Alannah grows anxious, studying each person as quickly as she could while passing. She taps the woman she is following. "Are you the doctor?"

Looking over her shoulder slightly, the woman replies, "No. She will be in shortly to speak with you." Scanning her hand on a reader beside a door, the door slides to the left. The woman shows Alannah to the next waiting area.

Instead of sitting, Alannah causally paces around the room. She looks at the various paintings on the wall. Most of the paintings were abstract works, fused with something deeper that she was trying to make out. Like shapes of people and bodies. Yet it was so subtle and discreet that you would miss it if you didn't look at the work closely.

The sound of another nearby door opening startles Alannah. She had forgotten where she was, having been so focused on one of the paintings.

"Alannah?"

"Yes."

"Hi. I'm Dr. Helen Bantu."

The two shake hands.

"Please. Have a seat. And I will take that," The doctor reaches out for the small device.

Alannah sits after handing the device to the doctor. She crosses her legs and leans forward, ready to listen attentively.

"How was your drive here?"

"It was nice! Very scenic! But I almost couldn't find this place. It's so hidden out here . . . in the country."

Laughing, the doctor replies, "Yes. This location is mostly reserved for our special clients. Clients that need the upmost discretion."

"Oh, wow. But I'm nowhere near a special client," Alannah says, smiling innocently.

"Well, you are, actually. You called our facility from one of our client's listed phone numbers."

Alannah frowns a bit, but then quickly remembers that she did in fact do this.

The doctor continues. "This client has an important relationship with our company. They have arranged that anyone associated with them who shows interests in what we do here - be given special treatment."

"I'm confused," Alannah tilts her head a bit.

The doctor reclines in her seat. "Consider it a . . . visitor pass to an exclusive club."

"Oh, wow. So now what?"

"Well, at our other locations, we would ask you a bunch of questions. These include the type of men or women you are interested in, your hobbies, and/or what your sex life is like. But here we have a special process that we conduct to really find out what gets your blood pumping, so to speak."

Blankly staring, Alannah doesn't say anything.

"Interested?"

"I, um – hmm. Is it possible to get a preview of this *special* process? Can you tell me more?"

Rocking some as she thinks, the doctor finally replies, "Put this on and follow me." The doctor reaches into one of her desk drawers and gives Alannah her extra lab coat.

Leading Alannah from the room, the doctor exits the same door she entered. Following behind her closely, Alannah is in awe. The two walk pass similar rooms that Lincoln was shown during his orientation. Alannah is also shown the process, though she is shown much more.

When they approach a double set of glass doors, the doctor shows her identification to a special set of security guards. She scans her credentials and is allowed to bring Alannah in behind her.

The doctor escorts Alannah down a few hallways, leading her to an open area that had several doors. Each opened to individual rooms. The appearance of the area resembled the prison reality shows Alannah had watched from time to time as a teen. Though, these doors didn't have the inmates, violence or guards. Instead, there were various rectangular workstations with modern computers and devices. Some of these devices had wires that ran across the floor. All the wires were connected into wall panels. These panels were strategically placed beside the doors that lead to each of the individual rooms.

Whispering, the doctor says, "This is where we study the behavior of our clients. Our team reviews how our various clients respond to our technology, depending on their race, creed and color. This process ensures we get the highest compatible SINC match."

The doctor walks toward one of the doors, pressing a button. It opens a window that shows the activity inside of the room.

"Have a look," the doctor says, holding her hand toward the door. "Don't worry. They can't see you."

Hesitantly, Alannah crosses her arms as she walks toward the door. Peeking inside, she notices a woman sitting in a uniquely designed chair. The woman is blindfolded and naked. Pacing around her are various types of naked men and women. These people are doing and saying various things to her as they circle her like vultures over roadkill.

Stunned by the view, Alannah jolts backwards.

"Are you okay?" the doctor asks.

"Wow," Alannah says, slowly approaching the window again. To Alannah's surprise, the woman seemed to have been enjoying the activity. "Am I supposed to be seeing this? This is not what I expected when I asked for a preview."

The doctor gives Alannah a glance that answers her question. She opens another window before Alannah could finish looking through the first one. A similar activity is happening; though, this time it is only men. Another room has only women. In another room is a woman strapped to a table. Doctors are examining her responses to various phrases and touches.

"I – I don't feel comfortable with this," Alannah steps back from the last window shamefully.

"No? You seem quite intrigued."

Alannah sighs.

"Are you not interested in being fully compatible with your SINC? It will make for a much better experience," the doctor replies.

"I just want someone to talk to. Someone to keep me company right now. Nothing that I have to go through all of this for."

"Don't you have family or friends for that? Suiters? An attractive woman like yourself should not have any problem finding someone to keep her company."

"Attractive people go through their struggles, too." Alannah grows frustrated by the doctor's tone. "Do you have any other simpler option?"

Leading Alannah from the room and back towards her office, the doctor replies, "We have short-term options. But the risk of incompatibility is greater."

"What type of risks?"

"Well, for you – possibly none. You just want . . . to *talk* to our SINC. Others can expect physical enjoyment; although, we can't guarantee it will be enjoyable every time."

"Why not? It's just artificial intelligence, right? You can't program a computer to do exactly what you say?"

Sighing, the doctor replies, "If only it were that simple. This technology is not your simple, lower level programming. We program our SINCs to respond to our client's individuality. This process requires time and patience, testing. For those not wanting to experience this, we only have pre-owned SINCs. These SINCs have basic programming. They're not completely unique to your needs beyond your favorite color, foods, movie, etc."

The doctor stops in the hallway and looks at Alannah inquisitively. It's as if she was waiting on a response or another question.

"In a nutshell, the best match takes time. Look at it this way: most rushed relationships don't work out. Should a person not take time to really know their love interest, it goes south, right? Our process is like a transparent and patient relationship. It takes the necessary steps to stay intact for the long haul."

Alannah exhales deeply.

"It sounds like you are going through something right now. Because of this, you just need emotional support."

Alannah begins tearing up and nods her head rapidly.

"Okay. Tell you what I will do. I will give you a slightly modified but pre-owned SINC. It's not an immediate thing. It's neither as long of a process that I just explained. Does that work for you?"

"You would do that?"

The doctor agrees.

"Thank you, doctor," Alannah awkwardly hugs the doctor.

A bit annoyed by the embrace, the doctor pats Alannah uncomfortably on the back.

While at work, Lincoln gets a follow up call from a representative from SNAI Technologies. They were calling regarding his orientation. They were further inquiring to determine if he was still interested in pursuing a SINC relationship. After a heated, one-sided exchange regarding the racism he read about the company, Lincoln declines. The representative did her best to persuade Lincoln that what he had read and heard was untrue. But Lincoln stood his ground. Now, he was altogether turned off, unenthused and insulted by the presence of SINCs.

Not long after this call, Zeke rings Lincoln. He informs him of the information he obtained from the mystery woman's license plate. He was able to retrieve a home address. Zeke and Lincoln discuss it for a few minutes. Then, Lincoln agrees to meet Zeke in person for a drink to speak about it more.

Chapter 15

"I'm gonna go to her house. Simple as that," Lincoln says adamantly, sitting across from Zeke. They are speaking at another bar which they often frequent.

Zeke leans forward, resting his arms on the table. Looking around, he speaks quietly. "You sure that's a good idea? You could mess up and get caught. I could lose my job."

"How? How would they know you gave me her address? They won't know that. Ain't nobody going to jail," Lincoln taps the table emphatically.

Reclining, Zeke crosses his arms. He slouches some in his seat. He stares at some of the people in the room.

"You actually think I would rat on you?"

"I'm not saying that, man," Zeke shakes his head, clearly annoyed by the question.

"I would just say I followed her. I was at her job, right? So that means we met there. She saw me there." Lincoln fiddles with the coaster on the table. "Shit! She has been following me!"

"But you can't prove that."

"Yeah, I can. She was at the bar. The bartender saw her. And she paid for her drinks. There is a paper trail."

Zeke sighs. "Everyone is at a bar sometimes, Linc. Merely coincidence."

"I don't believe in coincidences."

A quiet overcomes the table.

"Just – just be careful, dude."

Lincoln leans forward. "Always."

"I still can't believe you considered getting one of those things, though," Zeke chuckles.

"Considered what?" Tommy approaches the table with two beers, one in each hand.

"Robots."

After placing the two beers on the table, Tommy takes a big gulp of his beer. The icy-cold beer bottles sweat profusely. "Oh, yeah. That's right. You still doin' that, Linc?"

Lincoln shakes his head and sighs. Scratching his face, he quickly changes the subject. "Where is Jake?"

"He's on that spiritual retreat, remember?"

"*Spiritual retreat*," Zeke says.

"Oh, yeah. Ain't nothing spiritual about that retreat," Lincoln smiles.

Zeke points at Lincoln, his beer in hand. "Right."

"He's just there to prey on some conflicted, religiously-confused booty," Tommy says.

"Shit, we do that here!" Zeke replies.

Boisterous laughter fills the table.

Alannah left her SINC orientation feeling confused, shameful and anxious. She immediately thought about Lincoln while driving back into town. Throughout their relationship they would take impromptu road trips to sightsee. They would stop at little mom-and-pop shops that still existed, purchasing freshly brewed sweet tea and lemonades to accompany home-cooked meals. Meals made from scratch by human hands. That process wasn't too common anymore.

They haven't bonded like this in a long time. The thoughts that arose during Alannah's drive to the Hills triggered her, and so she took a detour. She decided to go to the grocery store to see if she could find Exton again. Although, she hadn't any clue as to why she was doing this. Mixed feelings swarmed her mind, making her body feel like a warm blanket in the winter.

Alannah feels conflicted as she sits in the grocery store's parking lot. *Why am I here? What am I doing?* She thinks. Reclining in her seat, she commands the volume up a few ticks. She plays her favorite satellite R&B channel a bit loudly. Her emotions are all over the place. The next song featured on the playlist is Luther Vandross' "A House Is Not a Home."

Belting out some of the lyrics, Alannah sings," But a chair is not a house, and a house is not a home, when there's no one there . . . to hold you tight. And no one there . . . you can kiss goodnight." She sings this song with so much power that she tears up; so much so, in fact, that she doesn't notice a man slowly approaching her car from the left rear.

Tapping on the glass of her driver-side door, the man crouches so that Alannah could see him clearly. When he doesn't get any response the first time, he taps the glass harder.

"Oh, shit," Alannah says, startled upon noticing the man. She commands her window to roll down and does the same with the music's volume. "Hey – hey. What are you doing out here?"

"I should be asking you that," Exton says. "I was getting a snack across the street when I noticed you. What is this you're driving?"

Alannah doesn't know what to say. "Oh, a loaner."

"Oh, wow." Tilting his head curiously, Exton asks, "You okay?"

"I don't know what I am doing here."

"You wanna go talk?" Exton opens Alannah's door before she could respond.

Nodding, Alannah shuts down her car and gets out.

Walking back across the street, Exton leads Alannah into a bistro. They sit down at a small, two-person table against the wall. Caribbean music plays lightly throughout the place. Doing his best to lighten the mood, Exton dances some in his seat. He enjoys his snack while Alannah fights between looking at him and the menu. She eyes Exton closely, comparing him to Lincoln. Oddly, she also compares him to the SINCs she had seen not too long ago.

Exton is just as tall; maybe an inch or two more than Lincoln. He's a few years younger than Lincoln, and a bit more chiseled in his physique. The way his clothes fit turns Alannah on. It reminds her of the early days, when Lincoln would go out of his way to impress her with his style.

"What?" Exton asks, noticing Alannah eyeing him over the top of her clasped hands.

Shaking her head, she replies, "Nothing." She squeezes her legs together tightly.

"So, you want to tell me what's wrong? And why you were just sitting in the parking lot of my store? Singing like some old-school, *Showtime at the Apollo,*" Exton leans forward, sipping his drink. "You stalking me? Can I do something for you, Ms. Alannah?"

Removing her hands from her face, Alannah's slight smile disappears. "Wow! You went way back! My grandfather watched that show when he was a kid."

Exton laughs.

"Listen. About the other night . . ."

Exton clears his throat, interjecting, "Yeah, about that. I'm sorry. I was a bit forward."

"I'm a claimed woman."

"I know. But why are you here?"

Alannah exhales deeply, rubbing her brow.

"Doesn't seem like you claim him. Whoever he is," Exton continues.

"My relationship is complicated right now. We are working through it."

"That's fair. Does that mean we can't be friends?"

With a doubtful expression, Alannah replies, "Really? Friends? Do you always befriend people you can't have sexually nor romantically?"

Feeling defeated, Exton sits back in his seat. He glances at a television in the corner and watches an advertisement for a SINC. "You believe that it's come to this?"

"What?"

Nodding at the television, he replies, "That. People getting into relationships with technology and machinery. Our society is so attached to *things*. They think things will validate them or make them feel better. This world will end up not knowing real from fake."

"I think the world already has that problem," Alannah says, folding her arms. "Besides, I don't think they are so bad."

Exton leans forward. "Not so bad?! Are you kidding me?"

"Yeah. Some people just want companionship. Like the old lady who just needs assistance walking to store. Or the old man who needs help up the steps. The person who needs a meal cooked or wants to feel safe at home. Some technology is good."

"Some, but that . . ." Exton points at the television, ". . . is excessive. Wait. Wait a minute. You're into those things?"

"What do you mean?"

"Oh, shit! Have you been with one?"

"Not everyone uses them for sex. Some people just want company, sir," Alannah leans in to whisper.

"But those things . . . Alannah. They – they void the soul of real, tangible, human connection."

"No, they don't. Not for people who are emotionally stable and understand they are essentially dealing with a computer."

Exton shakes his head and rubs the corners of his eyes. "Anyway. You know what you want to order?"

Alannah nods.

Exton taps the table, causing a screen to appear with an automated menu. Alannah scrolls through the options, selecting a latte. Exton reorders another of what he had been drinking. Moments later, a waiter brings over their drinks.

"So, let me guess. You are either contemplating getting one of those robots, or know someone who has?" Exton asks.

Alannah says nothing. With her eyebrows raised, she sips her latte.

"Why pay money for that when you can have all of this?" Exton moves around in his seat as if he were on a dance hall floor.

Catching her off guard, Alannah laughs while sipping her latte. She laughs hard enough that she blows some of the drink all over Exton's face and shirt. "Oh shit! I'm so sorry."

"It's okay. Make it up to me." Exton grabs a napkin and begins to clean up the mess.

Putting her cup down, Alannah replies, "Make it up to you? How?"

"Let's go out."

Alannah chuckles. "Do you have amnesia all of a sudden?"

"C'mon! Just *this* – what we are doing here but again. And again, and again and again."

"Sir. I can't. Besides, I am going back to the Hills when I leave here."

"The Hills? Marlay? Nice! I can come out there. I've been to a couple wild parties out there in the past. People out there are into some weird shit, though."

Alannah shakes her head slowly. "I don't even wanna know."

"C'mon, Alannah. Just another harmless latte, but without it getting on my shirt next time."

"Another time, sir."

"See. Was that hard?" Exton smiles.

Alannah rolls her eyes. "I didn't agree to anything."

"True. But you didn't say no either."

Chapter 16

ALANNAH THINKS ABOUT THE BRIEF OUTING WITH EXTON while she drives back to the Hills. She's once again smiling but also feels guilty. *I shouldn't be toying with that man, but damn if it isn't fun. How did it come to this? Hanging out like I'm single,* she thinks.

A sudden beep from Alannah's car startles her, breaking her from her thoughts. Her messaging notification system had an alert for her. It was a video message from Sherrie.

"Show messages," Alannah commands the car's smart system.

A slightly transparent blueish square appears in the top left corner of the car's windshield. *Loading* blinks a few times. Then, the recent message pops up and begins to play.

"Hey girllll! Just wanted to make sure you were good! I gotta surprise for you soon! Like really soon!" Sherrie says, winking.

"What is she talking about? A surprise?" Alannah thinks aloud.

Once back at the house in the Hills, Alannah curls up in a large lounge chair and reads. The house is so quiet at times that it's unnerving to her. During these moments, she turns on the television just for some background noise. Doing this reminds her of being home with Lincoln. He would always have some show playing on television no matter what was going on in the house.

Without notice, Alannah falls asleep in the chair. The book sort of dangles on her lap. She had a weird dream that she was being covered in a fluid, and she was trying to pull herself out of it. The fluid was thick and heavy, though, and seemingly unmovable. At first no one comes to her aid after she reached and begged for help. But just as she was about to succumb to the thick glob that was pulling her down, a robotic arm pulls her out.

Suddenly the doorbell rings and awakens her. She feels disoriented after being in a deep sleep and believes the person at the door was Exton. *Could he have followed me? He said he was familiar with the area. But he wouldn't do that,* she thinks. Waking up a little, she follows the sound of the doorbell going off again. Thinking about it more, she says, *Get a grip, girl. Wake up.*

At the security panel, Alannah looks outside. She notices that it's the neighbor again. Holding a bag in his hand, he's looking around weirdly at the door, the window and the camera. Sighing, Alannah contemplates on what to do. Deciding to play it safe, she presses the speak button on the console.

"Yes?"

"Oh, hey again, temporary neighbor!" The neighbor looks up at the camera.

"Hello."

"Just wanted to see how things were going. A pretty girl like yourself being all alone – in such a big house. Thought you might need a hand or two . . . you know, with anything. I know this house like the back of my hand."

"No, thank you. I'm good."

"Are you sure?"

Alannah leans against the wall, annoyed. "Yep. About to work out, so I need to go."

"Okay, well here is a little gift for you. I will leave it right here on the step. Just a welcome to the neighborhood type of a thing." The neighbor leans down and positions the bag in the corner by the front door.

"Okay, thanks."

Waving, the neighbor walks away.

Alannah watches the security console as the neighbor makes it to the front gates, exiting the area. Something about him gives her the creeps. She wasn't sure if it was his long, narrow face with no facial hair, or his creepy eyes. After noticing him leave the premises, Alannah comes outside and cautiously looks around.

Sensing that Alannah probably had walked away from the security console, the neighbor stops just outside of the gate. He stands behind one of the large columns so that he couldn't be seen from the house, where he looks at the home oddly. It was as if he was waiting for something to happen. After several seconds, he continues to his ATV he normally used for traveling short distances near his property.

Looking back over his shoulder, he notices Alannah stepping outside and grabbing the bag. He smiles to himself, as he refocuses on the path in front of him.

Staring at the bag while on the front stoop, Alannah nervously inspects it. She doesn't know if she should keep it, open it, or toss it. Playing it safe, she tosses the bag in the trash can by the garage. But first, she made sure the neighbor was gone and couldn't see her doing this.

Back inside the house, Alannah grabs the book she had been reading, continuing where she left off. She casually walks around the house, passing by the SINC in the glass closet more than once. But this time, Alannah pays it no mind. The third time she passed it, she paused her reading to study the SINC closely. Since she had a behind-the-scenes look into the SINCs, she is even more curious on this SINC's personality.

What type of person is the owner? What did they tell them he or she wanted this SINC to do? She thinks.

Deep in her thoughts, the doorbell going off again both alarms and irritates her. *Again? What does he want? Did he see me throw that bag away?* She thinks, frustrated. Storming toward the front of the house, Alannah opens the door aggressively without looking at the security console.

"SURPRISE!" Sherrie screams, with Monica and Elina standing beside her. The three of them are holding something different. Bottles of wine, fruit and cheese platters, and a bag of food.

Alannah grabs her chest in shock. "What – what in the world? What are y'all doing here?"

"Well, we know you have been down recently . . . and being secluded in this big ole house isn't helping. So, we thought we would come hang out," Elina says, walking inside. She looks around the home and is awestruck by the tall ceilings and fancy floors.

"Oh wow! Y'all didn't have to do this," Alannah replies, closing the door behind her friends.

Monica inspects the foyer. "I just wanted to be nosy; see what this place is like after Sherrie told me you were out here. But . . . yeah. Let's go with what Elina said."

"You're stupid," Sherrie chimes in.

"But who is that creepy dude down the road? He stared at us something fierce when we drove by," Elina adds.

"He did?" Alannah folds her arms. "Can't say I'm surprised. He creeps me out."

"That's just the neighbor. He is suspicious about everyone coming through here. He thinks he owns this house," Sherrie interjects. "Did he come by here, A?"

"Yeah, more times than I am comfortable with."

Sherrie chuckles. "He's harmless, girl."

"ANYWAY! Onto a better subject! Who - of all things SEXY - was that the other night?! You weren't too forthcoming in the group chat about your boy toy at the lounge! And don't give us that nonsense about him being an *old co-worker*," Elina says excitedly.

Monica continues to inspect the house, now standing in the kitchen. She presses a button, commanding a cabinet full of dishes to open. She joins in the conversation, without breaking her concentration on getting a good tour of the place. "Mmm, hmm. And why is he kissing on an *involved* woman?"

"He knows I am involved."

"Oh, he does, does he? That makes this conversation even more interesting," Monica says.

"And he is still coming at you that aggressively?" Elina makes an unsure, surprised facial expression.

"Sounds like someone might be done with that *involved* title," Sherrie says. "It looked like you fully enjoyed his aggressiveness the other night."

Alannah sighs. "Can we change the subject? Can y'all get out of my business?"

"We got your back, no matter what you decide. But, um, if you don't want him . . . can I have him?" Elina asks, laughing. She leans on Alannah innocently.

"You are sick!" Alannah gently pushes Elina away.

The group enjoys a moment of quiet. Everyone either drinks, eats or roams the house.

Eventually breaking the silence, Alannah shouts, "Sherrie!"

"Hmm?"

"Why didn't you tell me about the robot in the closet?"

"THE WHAT?!" Elina peeks her head out from behind the wall in another room.

Sherrie mouths, "Robot?"

"There is a damn robot in the other room," Alannah replies. Without warning, she walks off down the hallway.

The group follows behind her closely, as if they were told that there was a wild animal in the house.

Pointing like a frustrated parent, Alannah shows her friends the glass closet containing the erotically dressed SINC. Alannah's friends stand stunned at the sight of the woman in the glass.

"Oh . . . my . . ." Elina covers her mouth.

Monica steps back. "Wow. I never thought I would see one of these in person." She rubs and grabs on her own breasts. "Did they have to make them so perky?"

Elina smacks Monica on the arm.

Sherrie walks around the glass, squinting her eyes as if she was a doctor inspecting a small wound. "A, I had no idea. I've never been this deep into the house. I know this thing probably scared you."

"PROBABLY?!" Alannah replies. "I called the police! Slept in the damn car!"

"Oh, wow," Monica shakes her head.

Elina looks at the automated lock on the container. "Did you open it?" Her voice is suddenly calm and almost unemotional.

"NO!" Alannah says. "I'm not messing with that thing."

"You don't want to try it out?" Elina asks.

Alannah stares at the glass hypnotically, forgetting to respond.

Stepping toward Alannah, Elina persists. "A?"

"Nope. I don't."

Chapter 17

LINCOLN GROWS FIDGETY SITTING IN HIS CAR, AS HE contemplates his next move. He's parked in front of a cluster of townhomes, one that has the address Zeke provided. In his mind's eye, Lincoln is flipping the tables by stalking the mystery woman. *But what am I going to say when I see her? What am I going to do when I confront this woman? Why was she following me?* He thinks.

Sitting in a visitor space not far from the home, Lincoln watches what appears to be the woman. She's walking around her home. The windows are slightly covered by blinds; although Lincoln has seen enough to feel ensured he is in the right place.

More than once, she comes outside alone, bringing bags and putting them into her car. Upon seeing her come out the third time, Lincoln gets out of his car slowly. He starts walking in the direction of her driveway. But he stops suddenly when he sees a small boy following closely behind the woman.

Lincoln decides to wait.

Turning around quickly, Lincoln gets back into his car. He waits for her to get into her car and leave her driveway. He follows her as she runs errands, stopping and waiting patiently as she goes into a couple stores. Eventually, she stops again. She drops the young boy off at daycare, while then driving to a nearby coffee shop.

Lincoln parks not too far away from her, watching her exit her car and go inside. He debates on confronting her in the parking lot. *She could easily get into her car and run again*; he thinks. Changing his mind, he walks a yard or two behind the woman and keeps out of her sight.

But then, he goes inside of the store. He gets in line a few people behind her, pretending to be a customer. After she orders her coffee and takes a seat, he abruptly sits down at the same table with her.

"Why are you following me?!" Lincoln aggressively whispers, wasting no time with introductions.

Realizing who was questioning her, the woman grabs her bag. She attempts to leave sharply, but Lincoln yanks at her arm hostilely.

"Unhand me, now, sir," the woman says with a stern, but calm tone.

Lincoln continues his interrogation. "Why should I?! Who are you?"

"Please. Let go of me," the woman says, maintaining her calm stance. She looks around, hoping no one is watching the altercation.

Lincoln stares at the woman intentionally, doing his best to get his question answered. "Wait - I remember you now. You work at . . . at the –"

"Please, shh," The woman covers her mouth with her index finger. "Yes. I do."

"Explain then."

"I can't say much. I am being watched, always."

Irritated, Lincoln replies, "Watched? By whom? Can't say much about what?"

The woman sighs. "The technology my company distributes is dangerous. That's all that I can say."

"The SINCs?" Lincoln rears back in his chair.

Looking around to ensure no one was listening, the woman replies, "Yes. I advise you to stay away and not pursue them." The woman gets up, leaving towards the entrance as her coffee was being placed on the table.

Lincoln turns around in his chair. "Wait, that's it?"

The woman stops briefly, turning her head to speak over her shoulder. "Tell your girlfriend, Alannah, to do the same. She could be in danger." The woman walks briskly out of the shop.

"Bullshit!" Lincoln screams loudly, standing. Everyone in the coffee shop becomes concerned. All turn to look at him. Running after the woman, Lincoln grabs her by the arm again and yanks her around. "If that's true, show me proof!"

"Ma'am are you okay?" A random patron steps toward the two.

"We are fine, sir. Thank you," the woman replies, awkwardly.

"Yeah. *FINE*," Lincoln agrees, eyeing the patron furiously.

Fiddling through her phone, the woman pulls up an order report. It had Alannah's name and the address in the Hills.

"I . . . this can't be true." Lincoln stares at the phone in disbelief. "But I still don't understand. Why are you are doing this? You can't tell me more?"

"About the company, no. But I can tell you this," the woman sighs. "My father died because of racist organizations like this one. I will do whatever I need to in order to bring this corporation, and others like it, down."

Shocked, Lincoln watches as the woman aggressively walks away. She doesn't say anything else. It was as if he couldn't move from where he was standing. After a moment, he gets inside his car. Leaning back in his seat, he replays everything the woman said.

Are you serious? How could she? How could Alannah do this to me? He thinks. Grabbing his phone, he wants to call Alannah. Though, he doesn't.

Across town, Zeke is lying in bed. His arms are behind his head. His eyes are closed and there's a slight smile on his face. He moans every so often, responding to the extraordinary attention he was getting now. Whenever he would open his eyes, all that he could see were the bedsheets moving up and down. It was as if they were attached to a string being pulled rapidly toward the ceiling.

"You like that, baby?" a woman says from underneath the sheets.

Breathing heavily, Zeke replies, "Mmm, hmm."

Coming close to climaxing, his phone begins to ring. He ignores it at first, pressing the decline call option without looking at the phone. The phone rings again. He responds the same way. By the third time, Zeke grows frustrated after having lost his concentration. He answers the phone without looking at who was calling.

"WHAT?!"

"I CAN'T BELIEVE THIS SHIT!" Lincoln screams into the phone.

"Linc?" Zeke pulls the phone from his ear and looks, ensuring he was talking to the right person. Sitting up, he yanks back the sheets and pushes the woman out of the way. He gets out of bed and goes into the bathroom. Whispering, he continues, "Shit, what happened?! Please tell me you didn't mention me."

Outside of the bathroom, the woman shakes her head in frustration. She flops down on the bed and stares at the ceiling as she listens to Zeke's muffled conversation.

On the other end of the call, Lincoln complains aloud to himself. He finally responds, "Nah, nah, nah. Man – just meet me at the pool hall later."

"What happened?"

"Just meet me, man!"

"Okay, okay. What time?" Zeke asks. He texts Tommy separately while on the phone with Lincoln.

Linc doesn't sound good. Meet at the pool hall later.

Moments later, Tommy replies that he would meet them there after work.

Lincoln replies groggily to Zeke's question. "Doesn't matter on the time. I will already be there." He hangs up without saying anything more.

A half an hour later - after sitting in his car in the pool hall parking lot with his anger festering - Lincoln goes inside. He sits at the bar. Eventually, he calls his job to tell them that he wouldn't be in today. The bartender brings over his usual drink and is surprised to see Lincoln so much earlier than usual.

"You okay, Lincoln?" the bartender asks, her eyebrows raised.

Rotating his glass on the bar top with his fingers subtly, Lincoln nods to the bartender's question. He stares at his glass for a few moments without partaking. After taking one small sip, he puts his glass down. He then leans back against his chair, folding his arms. He watches the sports highlights on the television, shaking his head at the assessments the commentators made about various sports events.

While enjoying the background chatter, Lincoln is startled by the presence of a random patron. A woman - a bit older with subtle, flowing gray streaks in her hair - taps his shoulder. She looks to be in her late forties or early fifties.

"Anyone sitting in these seats?" she asks, pulling the chair from the bar without waiting for a response. Wearing a fitted business dress, she seems anxious and flustered.

Lincoln is a bit on edge from random people approaching him lately. He only shakes his head and continues to watch the television. But still, he moves over a seat as a precaution.

"Wow. I don't bite," the woman says, smiling.

Lincoln smiles, but doesn't say anything, Instead, he stares at the television. Every so often he would glance at the woman subtly, especially while she was distracted from reading the menu. He was oddly turned on by her, as he discreetly studied her long hair, wide hips and thick thighs. She sat with almost perfect posture at the bar. Lincoln wondered if she was waiting on someone else to show up.

"Can I get a Jameson on the rocks?" the woman asks the bartender.

The bartender nods. "Coming up!"

Speaking to the woman without looking in her direction, Lincoln says, "Already that bad today, huh? Join the party."

"Right. I think I just bombed an interview," the woman replies. "I started rambling and overshared, and I spilled my coffee. Just so damn nervous. I prepared for it and everything!"

"I've been there. Don't worry too much about it. You probably did better than you think."

The woman briefly smiles at Lincoln's comment.

Lincoln introduces himself. The woman does the same. Their conversation continues long enough to where the woman moved a seat closer to him. At times, her legs would brush up against his. An hour later, both had already had two more drinks each. They were now facing each other, talking and laughing as if neither were concerned what was on the other's mind.

Enjoying the laughter, the woman accidentally knocks her bag onto the floor. It had been hanging on the arm of her chair. Simultaneously jumping down to get it, both Lincoln and the woman reach for the bag, but then, they come face to face to each other while kneeling near it. Staring at each other deeply, both Lincoln and the woman aren't sure what to do next. Clearing his throat, Lincoln thinks, *Fuck it.* He goes in for a kiss.

Zeke and Tommy then walk into the venue, after showing their drivers' licenses at the entrance. They laugh at a conversation they had on the way in.

"Something's wrong with you, man!" Tommy says, hardly containing his laughter.

"I'm just sayin', Tom. Catfishing should be a thing of the past since we have all the technology that we do now. This chick had the nerve to show up the other night - a hundred pounds heavier. That's bullshit!"

"I still can't believe you just *walked* out the spot."

Zeke's eyebrows touch the top of his face. "What was I supposed to do?"

"You could have been a gentleman and finished the date at least," Tommy replies.

"Mannn, no. That's wastin' both our time."

Tommy strokes his chin. "Shit. She wasted y'all time as soon as she put old photos on her profile."

"EXACTLY! Talkin' 'bout she gained a little weight from being too busy to work out.' Was going on and on about her career. No job is more important than maintaining my mental health and boyish figure," Zeke says, flexing his bicep.

Tommy shakes his head.

Both continue their conversation. They come around the corner of the bar just as Lincoln and the random woman were finishing their kiss. But now the two are standing, having been so hypnotized by the moment that they didn't seem to care who might have been looking at them in the room.

Stopping in his tracks, Zeke taps Tommy. They watch the display wide-eyed. Tommy covers his mouth in shock.

Opening one of his eyes, Lincoln notices his boys watching the action. Quickly he pulls away from the woman. "Oh, shit. Um – yo, what up?!"

Upon noticing the two strangers staring at her, the woman quickly grabs her things. She puts her bag strap on her shoulder, reaches inside of it and pulls out a business card. "Call me. Let's finish our talk,' she says, handing the card to Lincoln just before walking away, embarrassingly.

After the woman leaves, there was awkward silence for a few seconds. Then, Zeke spoke. "Talk, huh? So let me get this straight. You had a beautiful girlfriend, but for some reason . . . you wanted a robot. But now you're kissing older women in the pool hall. Or was that an old robot? Dude, did you buy an old robot?"

"Do those robots even have an age? Can they age? Or are they like vampires?" Tommy chimes in, laughing.

Laughing as well, Zeke continues to joke. "Linc, I know you are into some wild shit, but vampire robots are an all new high - even for my standards."

Frustrated by the jokes, Lincoln ignores the comments. He begins walking toward the area in a corner he and his friends normally frequented. It had his favorite table.

Speaking over his shoulder, Lincoln replies, "Man, shut the hell up and let's shoot."

Chapter 18

Alannah shakes her head as she listens to news streaming from her laptop. She exhales, relieved at the latest reporting:

BREAKING NEWS. A suspect has been apprehended for the alleged string of burglaries in Central Fellington. A representative for the CFPD has stated that the alleged suspect had been using his personal, customized SINC to assist him with these planned, tedious burglaries. Several in which brought him thousands of dollars in money and goods. For those who are unfamiliar, SINC is an acronym that stands for Sexually Intelligent Neuro-Robotic Companions, which is an artificial intelligence 'on steroids' as the manufacturer of these has said in the past. Customers usually acquire this technology for personal, intimate pleasure. Although, it seems as if this suspect had other things in mind for his. We spoke with SNAI Technologies about these events, and a representative for the company has spoken against the use of their technology in such a way. They are working on improving their programming to ensure this will not happen again. They are also beta-testing new security features. More on this at eleven.

"At least one thing can get back to normal, if I ever go back home," Alannah thinks aloud, gazing out of the window. She glances at the land near the rear of the home. The winding hills, thick foliage and tall trees.

Alannah's phone startles her as it rings. There's no name associated with the number and the word 'private' blinks.

Answering the phone hesitantly, Alannah says, "Hello?"

"Hello. This is the fulfillment department with SNAI Technologies. Is this Alannah Laghari?"

"Yes. It is."

"We are going to send you a text message. If you could, please confirm your identity by typing in the four-digit pin you used upon establishing your account when you receive the text."

Alannah waits a few seconds for the text to arrive. Upon receiving it, she entered the details as requested. The representative gets an alert that Alannah completed this step.

"Thank you. And your street address that you used for the order?" the representative asks.

Alannah recites the address, as if she had been living in the home for ages.

"Thank you. The reason for calling is to inform you that your order is ready."

Freezing up excitedly, Alannah doesn't reply right away. She had been so consumed over the past couple of days that she had almost forgot about her SINC orientation and the order she had placed.

"Hello? Ms. Laghari? Are you there?" the representative asks.

"Uh, yes. Yes. Sorry. In the middle of working, and – um. Okay. Thank you for the call."

"Wait, wait. We need more information from you. Would you like to pick up your order or have it delivered?"

"Um, delivery. But can you delivery it after hours? Like, when it's dark?" Alannah asks uncomfortably. Although Alannah is not at home and nobody around here knows her, she still feels shameful for making the purchase.

"Don't worry, ma'am. Our delivery team operates at the upmost discretion. Your order will not be marked in any way. Nor will our drivers or delivery equipment. We can only deliver your order between our designated hours for the day you choose. We have as early as tomorrow available."

Alannah only had about a week left of housesitting, which meant a little less of that time to enjoy the SINC. Clearly, she couldn't take it home with her. *But am I ready to go back home?* She thinks. Alannah hasn't talked to Lincoln within a few days. Moreover, she has been out of the house. This has been the longest they had gone without discussing their relationship. Even after the miscarriage, they would somehow communicate.

"Tomorrow is fine," Alannah says dryly, after clearing her throat. Hanging up the phone after giving the representative a few more details, Alannah paces throughout the home again. She stops to look at the woman in the glass, wondering whether if moving forward with the SINC was the right choice. She had never felt so unsure and wishy-washy in her life. Crossing this line made her feel as though there were no coming back.

When her phone rings again, she returns to where she was working. Wondering if it was the company calling about her order again, or if it was Chase from work with good news, Alannah was shocked to see the word 'Mom' blinking on the screen. Hesitantly Alannah picks up the phone, but it takes her a moment to answer the call. Since Alannah had been so overwhelmed with everything, she hadn't called or spoken to her mom in weeks. Mostly because her mother traveled a lot with her new boyfriend. The most she heard from her mother was the usual text - 'Off to someplace' and would be gone for X amount of time. 'Love you.'

Alannah's mother had become high maintenance. She was very spoiled, selfish and often had a stubborn demeanor. It was primarily the reason she and Alannah's dad split many years ago. Though they never got divorced. They both moved on with their lives, even though they had stayed married and legally connected to each other. Sometime later, Alannah's father died suddenly from a severe seizure. Her mother received all his life insurance money and his assets. The soft, submissive woman Alannah had once known as her mother had exited. A new and more assertive person took over. Now she was dating younger men, often twenty years her junior.

"Hey, mom," Alannah finally answers the phone.

"Haven't heard from you, my child."

Alannah bites her lip, scrambling for a reason as to why she hadn't called. "Been busy with work. Where are you now? Greece again?"

"No. William surprised me with a trip to Belize. You need to get yourself a man that does things for you like this. Instead of -"

"I'm happy with Lincoln, Mom," Alannah interjects, wondering if she was being honest with herself at this point. "Daddy took you places, too. Stop pretending like he didn't. He showed you things you hadn't seen before. Admit it. You make it seem like you were so unhappy, and these new men have come to rescue you."

"What he did was move us into debt. It showed me what stress looked like. But he made up for it later."

Alannah heavily sighs into the phone. "Daddy loved you, unlike the mess of men you seem to rotate through now. You made daddy's health worse."

"Don't be mean, Alannah. I'm only kidding with you. Sheesh. I know that he loved me. Even your father would have laughed at my joke. I figured you would at least take after him and have his sense of humor. After all, you don't seem to like any of my traits. If you want to be honest about YOUR FATHER, he had his share of excitement without me. Stop acting like he was innocent. But anyway. Just wanted to let you know I'll be out of the country again. I'll be gone about a week if you need me. Call to check on me when you aren't running behind what's-his-face."

"Lincoln, mother. My boyfriend's name is . . . Lincoln," Alannah says, after thinking about Exton. "Have fun." *And stay there, please*, she thinks.

Back at the pool hall, Lincoln shoots a few rounds with Zeke and Tommy. Lately Lincoln's behavior has created tension among the group. Jake has finally shown up, after having gotten back from his retreat late the night before.

Clearly Lincoln was in a mood. Everyone was okay with not saying anything for a while. All talked amongst themselves about anything they felt comfortable sharing.

"I'm not sure what to do," Lincoln finally says, upon missing his shot. Exhaling heavily, he stands his pole in front of him and slightly leans on it. His cellphone buzzes. It was a call from Shelly, the pretty assistant. He ignores the call.

Jake sips his beer before chiming in. "Somebody catch me up. So . . . Alannah is messing around with a robot?"

"Jake, man – c'mon," Tommy says, holding out his hand.

"What? I'm tired of beating around the bush. Can we just be direct?"

"He's right, actually," Lincoln interjects.

"Huh? I'm sorry. Come again? Jake is what?" Zeke holds his hand to his ear, jokingly.

Sitting on the edge of the table, Lincoln continues. "I think she is only doing this to fuck with me. To make me jealous."

"Why would she do that?" Jake asks. "Aren't we too old for them type of games?"

Shaking his head slowly, Lincoln sighs. "She came home a couple times when I was out. I had left the information about the SINC on the table."

"Damn, Linc. So, she knows —" Tommy scratches his head.

Lincoln interrupts. "She *knows* that I was at least interested in learning more about them. But that's it."

"You see that? You see how worshiping false idols can ruin relationships? Technology is a bitch. All this artificial intelligence, robots and social media need-for-validation bullshit," Jake says.

Zeke moves around the table, as he leans in to make a shot. He rests his left hand on the table, gently gliding the stick with his right hand a few times to ready his stroke. After doing this a few times, he pushes his right arm forward. He hits the cue ball to drop the eight ball in a side pocket. "That retreat made you worse, I see."

Smirking, Jake gives Zeke his middle finger.

Sitting on a stool nearby, Tommy clears this throat. "He's got a point, though."

"See what happens when I leave for a few days? My flock has gotten lost. Fear not. I am home and have not forsaketh you," Jake chuckles.

"If you don't shut up, Jake … I am going to take off my belt and whoop you like your parents should have." Tommy says, grabbing at his waist. "Linc, how do you know for sure about this? Maybe she didn't see the information you said you had left out."

Glancing over at Zeke, Lincoln then turns back to Tommy. "Someone at the company told me Alannah placed an order."

Zeke gazes at the floor, listening.

Tommy takes a sip of his drink, swallowing before speaking again. "And you believe this person? Why would they do that? Better question: Why in the world would Alannah do this? She loves you!"

Lincoln scoffs. "Hmph. Loves me." Scratching his head, he continues. "But, yeah, I do believe them. There is something more happening with those SINCs. I was told to stay away from them. They aren't what they seem. I think the person might be on a mission of some sort. They are trying to tell as many people as possible, so that everyone knows the truth about these things. And maybe – I'm guessing – *maybe* . . . me and Alannah are one of the first people she felt compelled to tell."

The heaviness of Lincoln's words quieted and nearly froze the group in their respective positions.

"SEE!" Jake exclaims, slamming his hand on the edge of the pool table. Everyone in the area but Lincoln jumps.

"DAMNIT, JAKE!" Zeke and Tommy say in unison.

"Linc, I can't speak on all that. But I think you need to go get your woman. Go before technology contaminates your relationship further," Jake says, his tone becoming serious.

Thinking carefully, Lincoln strokes his brow.

Chapter 19

PACING THROUGH THE HOUSE THE NEXT DAY, ALANNAH IS antsy. She can't relax, so she looks out a front window. At times, she looks at the security console while impatiently waiting for her SINC to arrive. *Was she excited, scared, nervous or ashamed?* She couldn't figure it out. Nonetheless, she was tired of waiting. Those three- and four-hour delivery estimation windows were the worst.

Why couldn't they just pick a time and be there AT that time? She thinks. Even with all the technological advancements, delivery people still couldn't be prompt.

Sometime later, Alannah walks through the home and does various things. She makes the bed, puts dishes away and plans out her next meal. She walks past one of the tall, rectangular windows. As she did, she noticed the neighbor outside who stood on the opposite side of the security fence. He was oddly trimming one of the many tall shrubberies lining the fence on his side which faced his home.

"What the . . ." Alannah thinks aloud. Storming outside, she almost fell over one of the steps. She crosses her arms while approaching the gate. Speaking aggressively to the neighbor, she says, "Hey! What are you doing?"

"Hey, pretty house sitter. Seems my buddy went out of town again. He didn't set the scheduler for these hedges to be trimmed. They were getting kind of tall and wide. I'm sure you wanted to be able to see out here – all this pretty land and all." The neighbor continues to manually trim the hedges.

Eyeing the man suspiciously, Alannah momentarily walks away and goes to the garage. On a panel inside of the garage were several options to review and adjust the house's landscaping. The neighbor was right. The schedule option for automatic hedge trimming was set to 'off.'

Walking back to the fence assertively, Alannah says, "Listen . . . I appreciate your help, but I'm good. Please stop popping up like this. You are making me uneasy."

Stopping the trimming, the neighbor comes closer to the gate. "Oh, really? Well, damn. I'm sorry. I didn't mean to make you feel uneasy. I'm just helping out." Looking around, the man clears his throat awkwardly. "I've lived in this area for a while. Seen this land before these homes were built. Made some good friends with my fancy neighbors."

"What is it exactly that you do to afford living out here?"

"Oh, a little of this and a little of that. Investments," the man replies.

As the neighbor continues telling his story, Alannah notices an all-black, sleek delivery truck driving slowly down the road in the distance. Its brakes squeal a bit as it slows. The driver seems to be checking the addresses on the gates of the street's homes.

Alannah realizes that her order was about to be delivered, and she didn't want the neighbor to be there when it happened. "Oh, okay. Well, listen. I really appreciate you wanting to help. But I got this. I will schedule the trimmer."

"You sure?"

"Yep! I love doing yard work. I might just do these myself. Most people are so quick to hit a button to get things done. Nothing like good old-fashioned work." Alannah does her best with the neighbor, trying to give any excuse so that the man would leave. "The owner left a long list of things for me to do. Maybe I just haven't gotten to this task yet."

"Ah! Okay. Well, I apologize again. If you need anything or would like for me to help - let me know!" The neighbor walks away towards his ATV. He straps down his tools. Then, he starts up the ATV and drives away rapidly. Dust from the ATV wheels fills the air.

After he is several yards away and out of sight, the delivery truck pulls in front of the house. Alannah nervously stands in the doorway. She presses the button to open the gate before the delivery guy rang it.

Then, she runs down the front stairs toward the large, round driveway. Alannah points to the side of the house where it was more shaded and discreet.

"Please bring it in on that side. There is a path that leads to the back door." Alannah says, waving at them hurriedly. She quickly runs back in the house and opens the door at the other entrance.

Just as the wide doors slide open, a delivery technician approaches her. He wears only black clothing with no logos or markings. Without providing any greeting, the technician clicks around on a small tablet and asks, "Alannah Laghari?"

"Yes."

"Please type the PIN you provided here, confirming the delivery. And the last four digits of your phone number here." Three other technicians are standing behind the lead, positioned near the rear of the truck.

A confirmation dings on the small tablet. The first lead technician turns, nodding over his shoulder at the rest of his team. One of the other three technicians nods back, turning to the door of the truck that had a small keypad. Quickly, he enters his own code which releases the lock and latch on the truck's rear door. The door begins to slowly retract.

Hearing the sounds, Alannah's heart rate increases. She watches the door move up slowly. She hadn't felt this much excitement since . . . waiting on her pregnancy results. Or the first time she had sex with Lincoln. Or . . . Alannah's mind runs wild for several seconds until the truck's door is completely retracted.

Inside of the trailer, there is a blue hue to the small space with a foggy mist in the air. From where Alannah stood, it appeared like a smoky room in a nightclub environment. Or something out of the movies. A narrow, rectangular glass box was in the middle of the trailer, like the one inside of the home. But this box had frosted glass and was slightly taller. It had to have been around seven feet.

"Oh, my goodness," Alannah thinks aloud.

"What you're looking at, ma'am, is essentially a portable refrigerator. We must keep the technology you ordered at a certain temperature for the delivery. Otherwise, we could risk some sort of malfunction. Once the box is inside, it shouldn't take long for it to reach room temperature. You will know it's reached the correct temperature when this card reveals a barcode. At that point, scan the barcode on the card. Enter your PIN and you will be given instructions." the lead technician says. He hands Alannah a thin, black card that looks like a credit card. As he speaks, the rest of his team move and maneuver the glass box into the home.

Temperature? Why does a walking, talking computer need to have a correct temperature? Alannah thinks.

Once inside the home and standing in the hallway, another technician shouts, "WHERE YOU WANT IT?" He studies Alannah's body, raising one of his eyebrows at what he sees.

"Oh, oh – sorry!" Alannah jogs back inside the home, pacing the closest hallways. She isn't sure where she wants to put the box. After all, she has been having mixed feelings after ordering the SINC in the first place. *What if someone sees it?* She thinks, fearing being judged. "Put it right here," she finally responds, pointing to the guest room she had been using.

The technicians use a modernized, advanced dolly to roll the fragile box from out of the truck. They move it into the house and position it where Alannah wanted it. Then, the technicians press a button to command the dolly to lower the box to the floor. They press another button to have it detach from its base. At this point, the technicians attach a power chord to a special area at the box's base, plugging it into the closest wall outlet. Like how the other SINC in the home was positioned.

Alannah grows anxious. She is still unable to see her creation inside of the box, due to the special chemicals to keep it intact during delivery. The chemicals made the contents of the box blurry. "How long will it take to be ready?" she blurts out, embarrassingly.

"As long as the temperature in the home doesn't drastically change, it shouldn't take more than an hour or two." The lead technician replies, pulling out the tablet once more. He hands Alannah the tablet and points to it. "Please digitally sign your name here, here and here. And type your PIN here."

Upon completing the last steps, Alannah hands the tablet back to the technicians. She watches as the group leaves without saying anything more. Locking the doors, Alannah arms the house just before returning to the room with her SINC.

Down the road, the suspicious-acting neighbor sits on his ATV. He watches as the unmarked delivery truck drives by.

Alannah curls up in a large and soft armchair in the corner of the room. She watches her creation slowly unthaw. Holding the card tightly, she glances at it impatiently. Her leg bounces nervously. Eventually she falls asleep.

Sometime later, she bats her eyes slowly as she awakens from an unplanned but much needed nap. Focusing her eyes, Alannah sits up. She is startled but excited. Her SINC was completely thawed. It seemed to be staring directly at her. Hesitantly, she gets up from the chair. She folds her arms tightly as she walks toward the box. Alannah inspects the SINC closely through the glass, like a patron at a museum of rare artifacts.

Stunned by the sight of it, Alannah covers her mouth in awe. The SINC was almost exactly as she wanted it to be, despite not going through the more strenuous build process. The doctor took the questionnaire that Alannah had completed and created her ideal man as much as she visually could.

Standing at six-foot-four, the SINC had a dark brown complexion. It had short, curly hair and broad shoulders. It had a goatee with a chinstrap beard, with subtle freckles around its cheeks and nose. The SINC was casually dressed in fitted jeans and a button up shirt with the sleeves rolled up slightly. No-lace casual shoes, and one stud earring in its left ear.

Standing with perfect posture, the SINC had his head tilted downward slightly. It appeared as if he was modeling for a magazine. Alannah moved in front of it, staring into its brown eyes. She examined its smooth skin and facial hair. Alannah wasn't a fan of big, thick beards. She was amazed at how real the SINC looks, just like the other one in the house.

Eventually Alannah looks at the card in her hand. The technician had stated that a barcode would now be revealed on it. Building up the nerve, it took a few minutes for Alannah to move further with the process. She paces around, exhaling at times. "Just do it, Alannah. It's here now," she thinks aloud.

Using her phone, she scans the barcode. Seconds later, an app appears on the card that asks for her PIN. Once she enters the number, Alannah is taken to a simple page with a few steps. The first step requires her to activate and register her SINC. Next, she must say her name and some other phrases a few times. Therefore, she could activate the SINC's built in voice-recognition security.

The final step required Alannah's handprint, which she had to register on the SINC's back. Should the SINC's voice recognition not work, Alannah's handprint would operate it as an optional failsafe. Entering her PIN on the glass box's small keypad, Alannah steps back. She heard a few sounds shortly before the box begins to open. A pleasant smell comes from the box, almost reminding her of how new sneakers smelt when she was a kid. Alannah approaches the SINC slowly once it opened.

Uncomfortably, Alannah reaches out. She felt the SINC's arms and chest. Startled by how it felt, Alannah yanked her hand back. Its soft but muscular texture felt so real that she was in awe. She found herself turned on by the SINC's touch, mostly because of the size of the SINC's pectoral and stomach muscles.

Alannah snapped from her lustful gaze as she pressed a button. The round platform where the SINC was positioned turned so Alannah could reach its backside. Slowly lifting the SINC's shirt, Alannah ran her fingers up the SINC's back. She felt the firmness of its muscles and the curves of its shoulders. Closing her eyes, she began to feel aroused. For a moment, she hugged the SINC from behind.

With her hand on the SINC's back, she began the activation process. A blue light illuminated under her hand, blinking subtly. But before Alannah could leave her hand on the built-in biometric reader long enough for activation, her phone startled her as it rang. Alannah grabs it and flips it over. Lincoln had called. As much as she wanted to ignore him, her varying levels of guilt made her answer.

"Hey."

"Hey," Lincoln replies, clearing his throat. "Hey. Um . . . How are you?" Lincoln was fighting back his anger to maintain a reasonable tone. It was a battle he felt he was slowly losing.

Taking a few seconds to respond, Alannah replies, "I'm okay. You?"

"You know me, A . . . just chillin' mostly."

Alannah glances out of the window. She watches the trees move with the wind. "Been out shooting pool lately?"

"Yeah. Jake is back."

"And what's today's word?" Alannah asks, laughing mildly.

Lincoln chuckles dryly. "Same ole shit. What have you been doing? How is housesitting?"

Looking over her shoulder at the SINC, Alannah replies, "Nothing, really. It's fine."

Lincoln grows anxious while sitting at his desk at work. He grows annoyed by the small talk and doesn't believe Alannah's response. Sighing heavily, he says, "We can't stay apart much longer like this, A. We will never figure things out." It's taking everything in Lincoln for him not to mention what he was told.

Alannah doesn't reply right away. Quickly she replays all the fights, arguments and discussions that she and Lincoln had experienced over the past several months. The more she thinks about these moments and their relationship, the more she is okay with being away.

"You don't miss home at all? *Me*?" Lincoln continues.

"Don't do that. Don't make it like I haven't tried, Lincoln. Of course, I do. But when I was home, you weren't. Even when your body was present, your mind was always somewhere else. Never in my life have I felt lonelier than the past several months. And with a person right there beside me."

Lincoln clears his throat, aggressively standing up from his chair. He stares out of the office window.

Alannah can feel Lincoln's frustration. "Maybe next week we can get coffee. We can talk more about our relationship." She wasn't sure if this was the right thing to say, or if she truly felt obligated to do this. But she said it anyway.

"NEXT WEEK! NEXT WEEK! Are you serious?" Lincoln paces his office. "Why are you so nonchalant about our relationship suddenly?! Are you seeing someone else? Who are you fuckin'?"

"Lincoln, I'm tired. I'm not *fucking* anyone. You are so worried about the wrong thing."

"But —"

Alannah interjects. "Lincoln, I am not arguing with you. It seems as if our relationship has been on autopilot for a while now. I'm using this time away to figure out what I need and what makes me happy. I suggest you do the same. I will talk to you later."

Without waiting on a response, Alannah hangs up.

Chapter 20

ALANNAH STARES AT HER PHONE FOR A MOMENT. SHE wonders if she was a little too cold in her response to Lincoln. But she was honest about her feelings; something she hadn't been for some time. Something about being away – the partying, hanging with friends, Exton and the SINC – has rejuvenated her a bit. *Why does it feel so wrong, though?* She thinks.

Walking back toward the SINC, she pauses just before placing her hand on the center of its back, and beneath its shoulder blades. Where she placed her hand begins to light up softly, just before the sound of a soft hum. A blue glow radiates beneath Alannah's hand. It was as if a huge, blue lightening bug was underneath the SINC's skin. After a moment, the same shade of blue brightens a small square just behind the SINC's ear.

Without warning, the SINC activates fully. It stands up straight with perfect posture. Its shirt falls back into place, after having been lifted by Alannah. Startled, Alannah steps back cautiously. She watches as the platform rotates again. Now the SINC is standing facing her.

Turning its head to face Alannah better, the SINC speaks in an eerily direct and human tone. "Hello, Alannah." Its voice is deep and soothing. Only an octave lower and it would remind Alannah of the late-night radio hosts that her parents used to listen to when she was young. After speaking, the SINC takes two steps off the platform and onto the floor. With each step, Alannah backs up more. The SINC takes a few more steps, causing Alannah to back up again. She falls into the chair she had fallen asleep in.

"Based on your heart rate and breathing, my programming tells me that you are afraid. Are you afraid?" The SINC moves his head slowly as it talks, as well as moving one of its hands. Already programmed mannerisms connect with its voice's inflections, based on how it should respond when meeting human behavior.

Alannah freezes in the chair, unsure of how to respond. "Uh – I don't know."

"Don't be afraid. You created me, Alannah. I am here to do whatever you want or need me to do. I am here to please you. I will not hurt you."

Alannah stares at the SINC for a few moments. She's unsure on what to do next. She is stunned by how human-like it looks and sounds. Except for slight pauses in the SINC's speech, and everything else she was exposed to about it; she couldn't tell the difference between it and a human.

"What would you like for me to do?" the SINC asks.

Sitting up straight in the chair, Alannah scratches her face gently. "That's a good damn question. Now that I've got you here, I don't know. Shit."

"What's wrong, Alannah?"

"What the hell am I doing?" Alannah thinks aloud, burying her face into both of her hands.

The SINC looks around and back at Alannah. "You are communicating verbally with me, while sitting on a custom-made Glenvar Chaise Lounge chair. It is retailed at sixty-two hundred dollars."

"No, no, no . . . what I mean is -" Alannah sighs. "Wait a minute! Sixty-two hundred dollars?!" Jumping up, Alannah stares at the chair.

"Is everything okay, Alannah?"

Alannah sits on the bed, and stares at the SINC cautiously.

Stepping toward her, the SINC asks, "What would you like me to do?"

Alannah's mind races. Now that she has the SINC in her possession, she doesn't know what to do with it. She is walking a blurred line of feeling turned on, scared and guilty.

Saying nothing, Alannah walks briskly out of the room. She walks down the hall and into the kitchen. She is starting to breathe heavily again. Doing her best to relax, Alannah grabs one of her half-empty water bottles. Quickly she finishes it off. Pacing near the hallway, she hears movement.

Peeking down the hallway, Alannah notices the SINC's silhouette as it slowly walks toward her. But she could only see the dark outline of the SINC because of minimal lighting in the hallway. It appeared as if she was walking in a dark alley, and someone was moving slowly toward her.

"Alannah?" the SINC calls out, as it continues approaching her.

Alannah's mind races. The SINC's voice suddenly sounds different in her mind. She thinks about the guys on the corner by her house. She further considers the recent break-ins near her and Lincoln's home. The creepy neighbor in the Hills, amongst other things, are what she has always been fearful about. Women being kidnapped, drugged and raped. Anxiety begins to grasp her.

"POWER DOWN!" Alannah shouts as the SINC gets closer to her. "POWER DOWN!"

The SINC stops its movements abruptly.

Now overly emotional and nervous, Alannah jogs back to her room. She leaps onto the bed, crying. She buries herself under the heavy and oversized plush comforter. After she eventually falls asleep, Alannah has an intense dream from which she later awakens sweaty. Her nipples are erect, her mouth is dry, and her panties are wet.

In the dream, she was strapped down and being teased by someone, though the person's hand could be seen. The remainder of the person's body was hidden in the shadows of the room. A voice – like Lincoln's - was talking to her sensually. Without warning, the voice begins to yell. The person teasing her leans in aggressively and screams, 'IS THIS WHAT YOU WANT?!' The person's face was blurred abstractly, appearing quite villainous.

Awake now, Alannah reaches for more water. Even though she thought she had left it on the nightstand, Alannah realized she had left the other bottle on the kitchen counter.

Walking back down the hall carefully, the SINC is still powered down. Although, it looked like it was standing in a slightly different position than what Alannah remembered. Uncertain if it had moved, Alannah walks gently by it. She eyes it like it was a sleeping tiger she didn't want to awaken. Realizing that there was another SINC in the home, she quickly goes into the room where it was housed, unplugging the unit from the wall. She didn't need two SINCs to worry about.

Back across town, Lincoln can't concentrate on his work. The conversation with Alannah annoyed him. He was furious that Alannah would go behind his back and get a SINC. Worst yet, Lincoln was even more upset that she didn't come clean about it. *What else could she have been doing?* He wonders.

Grabbing his phone aggressively, he calls his father. A feeling had come over Lincoln that he had been sharing too much with friends. Who better to talk to than his pops? Although they didn't agree often about most things, he knew his father would give him a straight-forward opinion about his struggles.

"Sssooonnn!" his father answers, excited to get the call.

Lincoln rears back in his chair. "Hey, Pop."

"Uh, oh. You don't sound good."

Lincoln's first urge was to do what he had always done – deflect and pretend like he wasn't bothered about anything. But an overpowering burst of emotions hit him unexpectedly. "She won't come home. I don't know how to get her back. It's like . . . it's like she doesn't care anymore."

Lincoln's father first said nothing. He clears his throat, making sounds here and there to ensure Lincoln that he is listening attentively.

"I know I haven't been myself for a while. I just – I just don't know how else to be right now," Lincoln continues.

One of Lincoln's team members walks into the office. Then, he quickly turns around at the display.

"Okay, son. Slow down. Breathe a minute."

Quietly, Lincoln slows down to regain his composure.

"Did I ever tell you the story about when I pissed yo' momma off so bad that she left me?"

"No. Why did she leave you?" Lincoln leans forward, resting his arms on his desk.

"The why is beside the point. But how I got her back *IS* the point."

"How did you get her back?"

Pops chuckles a bit. "I sang to her."

"You what?!"

"That's right. I sang to her."

Confused, Lincoln replies, "But you hate singing. You won't even watch musicals because you said . . . you said that you 'like acting and singing like you enjoy your pickles and sandwiches – separate.'"

"Separate," Lincoln's father says the same thing, at the same time. "That's right. That's right. But guess what?"

"What?"

"Sometimes you must take a drastic measure for drastic results. Sometimes you must risk it all, even if it means failure. Because, in the end, it all would have been a learning lesson. I risked embarrassing myself to let your mother know that I was serious. That I loved her enough to embarrass myself."

Lincoln sighs.

"Go get your woman, son. She still loves you."

Exhaling, Lincoln feels a new wave of energy flow through his body. It was as if his father was the leader of a platoon.

Suddenly he had given him a new mission. A mission he was motivated to complete.

At this moment, Lincoln's phone buzzes. "Hold on for a sec, Pop." Looking at the phone, Lincoln notices he had a text message from a strange number. Puzzled, he clicked on the text message icon. 'PICTURE MESSAGE: DOWNLOADING,' displays on the screen. After a millisecond, two photos are shown. Both photos show Alannah at the club dancing with a man. Another photo shows the same man leaning in towards her quite intimately. Although the photos were kind of dark and from a distance – not to mention having been taken at a challenging angle – it looked as if Alannah was kissing the man. Only the back of the man's head was showing.

"Motherf-" Lincoln grew furious. His mission had taken a turn. "Pop, I gotta go. Love you."

"What happened, son?"

"I gotta go," Lincoln says, hanging up the phone and storming out the office.

Chapter 21

HOURS LATER, ALANNAH RELAXED BACK AT THE HOUSE IN the Hills. She sat sipping tea while reading a book on the family room couch. Alannah could still see the powered-down SINC from where she is sitting. She kept a close eye on it at times, still unsure whether it could power back on and move on its own.

Oh, to hell with it! She thinks. Getting up quickly, she walks to the rear of the SINC. She again places her hand on its back. While the SINC activates, Alannah doesn't wait for it to finish coming online. Instead, she goes back to where she had been sitting. Once she finishes her cup of tea, Alannah yells toward the kitchen, "Coffee maker. Fresh brew!"

The coffee maker gurgles, and Alannah watches as the SINC turns toward her. It walks purposely into the room.

"Hello, Alannah."

"Hello," Alannah replies, speaking with a direct tone.

A subtle, technical glow appears in its eyes. The SINC replies, "Are you still afraid of me?"

"No. I wasn't afraid of you."

Moving closer, the SINC asks, "Are you certain about this, Alannah?"

Frustratingly, Alannah closes the book she had been reading and replies, "Yes."

"Good. May I sit down next to you?"

She nods to the chair across from her. "You can sit right there. What is your name? Do you have one?"

"Based on my records, you have not chosen a name for me. So, I have been programmed to respond to whatever you like."

"Hmm."

Alannah's phone buzzes several times from the other room. "Shit. Soon as I get comfortable," she thinks aloud.

"Would you like me to retrieve your cellular device for you?"

"Um, sure."

Getting up slowly, the SINC walks from of the room, down the hallway and into Alannah's room. Moments later, it returns and hands the phone to her.

Three missed calls and multiple text messages from Lincoln all appear varying minutes apart.

WE NEED TO TALK.

WHY AREN'T YOU PICKING UP THE PHONE?!

THIS IS BULLSHIT, ALANNAH!

Sighing, Alannah slowly shakes her head. She scrolls through the messages. *Bullshit?* She hasn't any idea of the new information Lincoln has.

"Is everything okay, Alannah?" The SINC moves its head, doing its best to show sincerity.

"Yes. No . . . I mean, I don't know."

"Based on your body temperature and language, you are frustrated."

"Nothing gets past you."

"I'm sorry. I don't understand your response."

"Nothing. Yes, I am annoyed. Frustrated. Sad. Horny. YOU NAME IT!!"

"I know what frustrated and sad mean. But these two feelings conflict with each other. My records indicate that horny means to be aroused and/or sexually excited. How can one be frustrated and sad, while being horny at the same time?"

Alannah runs her eyes up and down the SINC's body. "Believe me, it's possible."

Standing, the SINC begins to slowly unbutton its shirt, displaying its chiseled pectoral muscles. "Would you like me to pleasure you, and to bring you some relief of your horniness, Alannah?"

"NO! No, no, no. I am just *feeling* this way. This doesn't mean I want you to do anything." Alannah repositions herself, exhaling nervously. Whispering to herself, she says, "Not yet anyway."

With a slightly confused look, the SINC sits back down.

"I'm going to run on the treadmill. I need to get some of this out my system. You . . . you stay right here." Leaving the room, Alannah goes down another hallway and moves down some steps. After changing into her workout clothes, she activates the treadmill and runs aggressively. The sound of her running echoes off the walls and up the stairs.

Listening to Alannah run, the SINC sits patiently and scans the room. Noticing the library of books nearby, it approaches the wall. Quietly it begins reading each title aloud. The SINC then looks closely at the artwork on the wall and the sculptures on the end tables. Sculptures of half-naked men and women, touching and holding each other sensually. Other abstract sculptures resembling the solar system are positioned in a cluster in the corner.

Upon hearing the treadmill slow down, the SINC turns toward the hallway. It stands perfectly still, moving only its head as it waits for Alannah to return up the stairs.

"Whew! I needed that," Alannah thinks aloud, glancing at the SINC. She notices that it's standing now. "What were you doing?"

"Waiting for you, Alannah. And exploring the plethora of books that you have in your library."

"Exploring? Did you read some of them?"

"I read all of them . . . while you were running. I stored each book in my database. Would you like me to read you a selection?"

"Wow, you can do that?"

"Yes." The SINC moves its head and arm, mimicking human behavior. "Tell me, which one is your favorite?"

At first Alannah does not respond to the SINC but instead walks close to the library. Breathing heavily, she folds her arms and tightens her lips. A towel hangs over her shoulder. Small beads of sweat roll down her face, neck and chest. "Um, too many here are good. I need to shower, so maybe later."

The SINC approaches Alannah from her side. Standing closely now, the SINC studies Alannah's breathing and the moisture on her body. "Alannah, are you okay? Are you excited?" Taking the towel from off her shoulder, the SINC begins wiping her neck and arm gently.

The touch sooths Alannah, reminding her of when she went on vacation with Lincoln. For their first anniversary, they enjoyed a five-day trip to an all-inclusive Caribbean resort. After spending a few hours on the beach — swimming, relaxing and drinking — the two of them showered together. Both pleased each other sexually in the shower. Afterwards, they continued thereafter on the large, plush king bed for hours.

"Alannah?" the SINC speaks again, snapping Alannah out of her daze.

"Hmm? Yes?" Alannah steps away from the SINC, embarrassingly. "No — no I'm okay. Just an intense run."

"Do you need anything? How can I meet your needs in this moment?"

Shaking her head shamefully, Alannah says, "Just a shower. I need to – I need to cool down."

"Would you like me to join –"

"NO! No, no. I'm okay." Alannah begins walking away. "Wait. You can get wet? Like, in the shower? You know what? Never mind."

The SINC stands perfectly still, still holding the towel. It watches Alannah traverse her feelings and emotions.

Yelling from the bathroom, Alannah asks, "How good are you at listening?!"

"I am programmed to perform at the highest –"

"Alright, alright! Power down!" Alannah closes the bathroom door, locking it. "Can't get a straight answer from robots, I guess."

Alannah begins to undress, peeling off her fitted workout clothing that seemed to be glued to her body. *Maybe getting that thing was a bad idea*, she thinks.

After a brief sound, the SINC powers down and freezes in place.

Pacing the main floor of their home, Lincoln replays the conversation he had with Alannah. He further ponders everything else that was said and done over the past few weeks between the two of them. With a glass of whiskey in one hand, he throws back multiple shots in just a few minutes. Shaking his glass subtly, he utilizes his other hand to scroll through the few pictures on his phone. All were provided to him by an unknown sender.

Lincoln studies the photos as if he had a microscope. Meanwhile, the anger inside him grows wild, as his imagination grows like jungle vines. Who was the man in the photo? Lincoln didn't recognize him from any of Alannah's events, their neighborhood, the stores or the nearby venue.

All he could hear in his mind were the words: *Go get her.* But they were no longer being said in the way his father had delivered them. Nor Jake. The voice sounded more monstrous and possessive, especially after he visualized what Alannah could be doing with the SINC. Sexual, vivid thoughts. From his point of view, she was already publicizing it.

No shame, he thinks.

Lincoln considered telling Alannah that he was coming to the house in the Hills; however, he didn't. He wanted to ensure Alannah would be home upon his arrival. Lincoln then contemplates on what he should do. After putting on his black jeans, a black hoodie and dark-colored shoes, he leaves for the Hills.

Chapter 22

ALANNAH REVISITS HER PHONE AFTER SHOWERING AND getting dressed. She notices a missed call, followed by a text message. Both were from Sherrie.

Hey girl! Got another surprise for you! We are on the way to see you! Call me back!

Alannah glances out a kitchen window facing the backside of the home, pondering, *We? Who is we? I will call her back in a few.*

Looking through the windows more, Alannah notices the wind has picked up speed. It causes the trees to sway a bit. The sky was darkening. A brief but deep rumble of thunder startled her.

"Well, there went my plan to sit outside and chill," she said to no one particular.

The SINC still stood where she had left it, powered down.

"Activate," Alannah says.

"Hello, Alannah," the SINC says, after lifting its head.

"Hello."

"Did you enjoy your shower?"

Surprised by the question, Alannah changes the subject quickly. "You said you were good at listening. I need to vent a little."

"I am here at your command for whatever you desire."

Leaving her phone on the kitchen counter, Alannah walked to the morning room nearby. Sitting on one of the lounge chairs, she waved the SINC to come over where she was. After pointing to another chair and commanding it to sit, Alannah began to vent about everything under the sun. She spoke about Lincoln and their relationship. The miscarriage. The fights and the arguments. Her upbringing and her parents, and the strained relationship she often had with her mother.

Listening to Alannah as best as it could, the SINC mostly said nothing throughout the conversation. Instead, it moved its head in accordance to how it was programmed – to mimic human behavior. Every now and then, it said 'mmm, hmm.' Therefore, it seems as if it understood everything being said. Occasionally, it asked Alannah basic questions based on her body language and elevated tone. It would ask: *Are you okay?* or *Aren't you angry?*

"No, no. I'm not angry. Well, maybe a little. I'm just tired." Alannah replies. She notices that it was almost completely dark outside. Certain lights that were programmed to automatically turn on illuminate. "Wow. It feels like I have been running my mouth to you for forever."

Unbeknownst to Alannah, Sherrie had called twice more to tell her she was close to the home in the Hills. But now, she was pulling up through the front gate and parking. The front sensors trigger, causing the home's security alarm to chirp.

"What is that?" Alannah thinks aloud.

"Based on my programming, it sounds like your security alarm indicator. Someone is approaching the front entrance."

"What?!" Alannah jumps up and runs to the kitchen. Without looking, she grabs her phone and runs to the security console. Upon reviewing the various video camera squares on the screen, she notices Sherrie's car parking. "OH SHIT! OH SHIT!"

The SINC follows Alannah's movement, turning its body and head. "Is everything okay? Would you like me to alert the authorities?"

"No, no, no! STOP ASKING ME IF I AM OKAY!"

"I don't understand."

"Listen, just – you need to come. Come back to the room with me!" Alannah stood in the hallway, waiting on the SINC. Pointing to the room she had been using, Alannah waits until the SINC comes closer. Then she says, "Go to your closet and power down."

"As you wish, Alannah."

Watching the SINC from the corner of her eye, Alannah quickly throws on some clothes. Then, she commands the blinds to close and for the lights to turn off. She finally shuts the bedroom door behind her.

Jogging toward the front door, she gets to it just as the doorbell rings. With an awkward, shameful smile, Alannah begins to greet Sherrie. Before the door is completely open, she asks, "What are you doing –" Unable to finish her question, she is shocked by what she sees in front of her.

Standing next to a smiling Sherrie are two men. Exton is on one side of her, wearing a button-up shirt and casual pants. Most of the top buttons undone. A bottle of wine is in one hand while a tray of wine treats is in the other. On the other side of him is another random guy, similarly dressed. He's leaning against the stair railing with his arms crossed. He is holding something in a bag.

Alannah doesn't know what to say. Quickly she grabs Sherrie by the arm, yanking her inside and slamming the door behind her. Therefore, Exton and the random guy with him could not do anything.

"What the hell, Sherrie?"

"What? We came to hang out for a bit. I called you like three times to let you know." Sherrie shrugs a little.

Pulling Sherrie away from the door more, Alannah whispers, "And you brought Exton?! Why would you do that? How did you even get his information?!"

"I'm sorry if I blindsided you, but you have really been on edge lately. I ran into him at the store. He asked about you. I remembered him from the club and how y'all were so cute together. I figured we'd surprise you."

Alannah sighs, folding her arms.

"The other dude is a friend he brought for me. Ain't he cute?!"

Sherrie's comments are met by a frustrated stare.

"Okay, okay. I'm sorry." Sherrie tugs at Alannah's sleeve. "But c'mon, A. Let's just chill and talk for a few. Drink a little wine and play some 'Taboo,' 'What If? or Drink!,' 'Dating 101!' or something. We came all this way. Pretty please?"

Saying nothing, Alannah walks away toward the kitchen. "Just for a little while." She glances down the hallway, ensuring that she had closed the door to her room.

The front door opens slowly, followed by a chirp from the security system. "Everything okay?" Exton says, peeking his head inside. "Didn't want to keep standing out here, looking suspicious at this big ass house."

"Yeah. Come in, guys," Sherrie says.

Walking into the home hesitantly, Exton looks around. He's awestruck at the high ceilings, luxury furniture and accessories. As he approaches the kitchen, he notices Alannah standing with her arms crossed in clear annoyance. "Um, your friend said you would be cool with this, but you don't look too pleased."

"Hey, I'm Jaeshon. Just call me Jae," the other guy walks up, interrupting.

"Oh, my bad. Alannah, this is one of my homies."

Alannah waves awkwardly.

Noticing a weird silence building amongst the group, Sherrie steps forward animatedly, "Let's drink!"

Calming down a bit, Alannah asks, "What did y'all bring?"

Exton smiles.

"Well, you know I got our wine. But Jae brought something special for us," Sherrie says, turning to look at Jaeshon.

"Oh yeah?" Alannah presses the button on the cabinet. It starts rotating the wine, liquor and shot glasses. "And that would be?"

"I got that new Moto Tequila," Jae says, enthusiastically.

"*Moto Tequila*?" Alannah repeats inquisitively.

"It's a Black-owned tequila."

"Oh, I heard about that! The one that combines traditional tequila with some secret African spices and ingredients," Sherrie says.

"Will knock you on yo' ass," Exton says, laughing.

"I'm good right over here, standing on my feet," Alannah replies. She thinks about the time she had last gotten shots, and how sick they made her feel the next day. She places several glasses on the counter.

Sherrie grabs the bottle from Jaeshon. Then, she walks over to where Alannah had placed the glasses. "C'mon, A. Just one shot!" She peels off the plastic from the top of the bottle and pops the uniquely designed top, pouring the same amount of tequila in four glasses.

Exton and Jaeshon grab their glass. Each waits patiently as Sherrie edges Alannah on.

Sighing, Alannah says, "Okay. Just one." She grabs her glass.

Together the four say almost in unison, "Salute!" All raise their glasses toward one another.

Driving rapidly, Lincoln makes his way to the not-too-distant house in the hills. Between the drinks at home and the mini shots he was taking throughout the ride, his mind and nerves were on edge. He wasn't thinking clearly. The only thing on his mind was bringing his woman home, even if that meant . . . forcefully.

Swerving at times and barely avoiding hitting other cars, a random call from Zeke was the only thing keeping Lincoln sober. Zeke was more nervous about unethically retrieving and providing the details of the mystery woman's home than he was Lincoln's state. His guilt prompted the call more than anything else.

"Hello?" Lincoln says, after hitting a button on the car's steering wheel.

Zeke clears his throat, replying, "Yo, man. You alright? Just checkin' on you." He lies on his couch, one arm behind his head as he watches television.

"Nah. Haven't been alright in weeks," Lincoln's drunken state has prompted him to be the most honest he had been in a while.

"Where you at? Lemme come get you. We can go somewhere to get a drink."

"Nah. I'm good, homie. Already had plenty of those."

"What? And you're driving?"

Lincoln doesn't say anything. Instead, he continues sipping on a travel-size liquor bottle. He looks down for a second and drifts into the other lane. When he nearly hits an upcoming car, the sound of the opposite car's horn refocuses his attention. It causes him to swerve back into his lane. His tires squeal loud enough to be heard over the phone.

"Linc, please pull over somewhere, man. If the liquor doesn't cause an accident and kill you, the cops *will* . . . when they pull you over."

"Not pulling over. It takes a while to get to where I'm going."

"Where are you going?

"To the Hills."

"And then what?" Zeke rises. He moves his legs so that he can sit on the edge of his couch, nervously.

"I'm going to destroy that damn robot. I'm going to bring my woman home." Lincoln hangs up, not giving Zeke a chance to respond.

"LINC! LINC!"

Chapter 23

A FEW DRINKS LATER, ALANNAH CAN FEEL HER BODY relaxing. As she sips wine from her glass, she begins enjoying her friend's company, despite the boundary Sherrie had crossed. She had some choice words for Sherrie, but she would have to hear them later. With the sight of Exton in close range, and the SINC down the hall, both were enough of a distraction.

Sitting across from Exton and Jaeshon, Alannah is curled up next to Sherrie on an opposite couch. The four of them have paired up to compete in a girls-against-guys digital Taboo match. The guys were losing badly thus far.

Using a small remote, Jaeshon points at the small electronic Taboo device. He clicks a button, bringing up the next set of cards on the television screen positioned above it. Just before Jaeshon does this, Exton turns his back so that he can't see the cards; however, he is still facing Jaeshon.

Before Jaeshon begins giving clues based on the card's words, he stops suddenly and turns toward Sherrie. "Hold up! Pause the clock." Jae says.

"Pause it, why?" Alannah asks, holding the digital clock.

"Care to make this interesting?" Jae says.

"What you mean?" Sherrie says, clutching her imaginary pearls. She has been eyeing the arms and hands of her date for a while.

Jae moves up a bit on the couch. "Let's wager the game. Losers gotta do something. Best out of three."

"What, like strip or something?" One of Sherrie's eyebrows arches.

"Nope! Y'all enjoy." Alannah interjects, getting up from where she had been sitting. "I'm getting more wine. You want some?"

"In a few," Sherrie replies, not taking her eye from off Jae.

Jae stares back at Sherrie seductively.

Breaking Jae's gaze, Exton elbows him. "What the hell is wrong with you?" he whispers. Hopping to his feet to follow Alannah, he says, "I will go with you."

Alannah rolls her eyes as she nears the kitchen. Exhaling heavily, she says, "Why are you here? And whose idea was this really?"

"Listen, I'm sorry. But I had to see you again . . . soon," Exton holds up both hands in front of him, apologetically. He takes a few steps closer to Alannah, looking over his shoulder briefly to ensure privacy.

Alannah leans against the counter and crosses her legs. She casually holds her full wine glass. "*See* me again? Why? What do you *really* want from me?"

Taking a few steps more to get closer, Exton replies, "I just . . . I just feel like we have a connection. Ever since I saw you in the store – and then the club – and at the bistro - I can't stop thinking about you. I think about you so much that it's like I need you just to breathe. You gotta feel the same, since you came looking for me. And you're okay with me being here now?"

Alannah takes a big gulp of her wine uncomfortably.

"Now, I know I shouldn't be here. I know you got a dude." Exton sighs. "But – but I ran into your friend. She recognized me. We talked for a minute. I pressed her to arrange something so that I could see you again . . . just to talk. Something like the club again. I didn't expect this. She said you would be cool with me coming here." Exton continues.

Shaking her head, Alannah doesn't say anything. She grabs another wine bottle and walks toward the back door. After opening it, she exits toward the rear deck. She curls up in an outdoor chaise nearby, glancing at the sky. The clouds thicken and darken.

Exton sighs as his attempt to explain himself seems to have failed. Following Alannah to the door, he stops at the threshold. "Can I at least just sit with you? Keep you company for a bit?" Before Alannah can respond, he comes over and sits next to her.

Alannah hesitantly shrugs. "For a few, I guess. Looks like it's going to rain any minute now. Y'all will probably need to get going. Tequila and wet roads don't mix."

Looking and feeling defeated, Exton sips on his drink quietly. Reclining in his chair more, he shifts his gaze at the clouds forming. He notices a particular cloud that stood out from the others. "Oh shit," he says, chuckling.

"What?" Alannah glances over at him.

"That cloud right there," Exton points. "It looks like – like the shape of a hand, giving us the middle finger."

"Stop playin'. Where?" Alannah leans over toward Exton a bit, trying to see the cloud from his vantage point.

Exton sits up some, leaning over to get closer to Alannah. "Right there."

Finally seeing the cloud, Alannah laughs. "Oh my god! I see it!"

Only a few inches from her face now, Exton's laughter subsides as he stares at Alannah sensually. Her teeth and smile captivate him. He inhales the scent of her body and the freshness of her newly washed hair.

Eventually noticing Exton staring, Alannah lowers her guard. She allows him to lean in more. Gently grabbing her by the back of her neck, Exton pulls her in closer and kisses her.

Back inside of the home, Sherrie and Jae decided to make good use of their alone time. Both had been kissing passionately on the couch. Moving his hand gently up Sherrie's thigh, Jae leans into her more to lay her on her back.

"Wait, wait, wait," Sherrie says, returning to an upright position. "Whew!"

A bit out of breath, Jae replies, "What? You don't want to?"

"Yes, yes. I do. But – "

"But? What's wrong?" Jae looks around the room quickly. "Let's have some fun in one of these fancy rooms. Gotta be like ten rooms in this house."

Sherrie pauses. "I have a bit of an early flight tomorrow. Need to get back on my end."

Stroking his face while gathering his thoughts, Jae says, "Well then, let's go to your place."

Contemplating for a moment, Sherrie replies, "But your boy? You're going to just leave him?"

"He's good. Trust me. I will text him and we will figure it out."

Thinking about what Jaeshon had to say, Sherrie gets up from the couch. She walks to the kitchen, hoping to find Alannah. When she doesn't find her, Sherrie notices the top of Alannah and Exton's heads through the back window. Noticing the two of them kissing, it was clear that they had broken the ice more. From where Sherrie was standing, Alannah appeared to be okay with Exton being there.

"Okay, um . . . . let's go," Sherrie says hesitantly, walking back to where Jae was sitting. "I will text Alannah from the car and you text Exton."

"On it," Jae says, standing.

"Cool."

Arriving to the general area of the house in the Hills, Lincoln drove slowly. He studied each house as closely as he could from the distance, not wanting to pass it. His phone service was spotty in the area, causing the GPS to become unreliable. Even with his careful inspection, he passed the house more than once because the storm had picked up. It further darkened the area enough to make it hard for him to see the house numbers from the road. Moreover, he hadn't realized that the numbers were posted on the gate instead of the homes.

Driving once more by a specific home, he also didn't notice that the outdoor security lighting had been activated. Two people were currently leaving from the home's front door. Although, he was too busy looking down another road and across from the house, making certain he hadn't taken a wrong turn.

After making one last U-turn, Lincoln returned to the same home. He arrived after the two people had gotten in their car and left. It had started to rain, making it even more challenging to see the car's model or its driver. Parking at the home's front gate, Lincoln gets out of his car. He gazed at it through the fence and knew he was at the right place.

His GPS finally readjusts at this moment. "You have arrived at your destination," it said. He could hear it even with the doors of the car being closed.

Now able to see the house's number clearly, and with the GPS's confirmation, Lincoln quickly runs back to his car. He pulled off the road and drove until he found a safe place to park. Therefore, he wouldn't be seen.

Finding a nook slightly in the trees, it appeared to be a makeshift emergency pull off. Lincoln parked his car there as if he was a pretend cop. Turning off his lights, he reclined his seat. He watched the home from this location, still drinking. From his vantage point, he would see anyone from the house if they were inside, and if they came on the house's left side for something.

Once comfortable in his seat, his mind began to kick out questions. *Was that Alannah leaving? Someone else? Who was the other person? Do I have the right house? What the hell am I doing out here?* He thinks.

Lincoln patiently waited, but eventually fell asleep.

Thunder rumbled and crackled interrupting the shared kiss between Exton and Alannah. Exton could feel the rain drops getting heavier on his pants. A flash of lightening lit up some of the hills in the distance.

Turning toward Alannah again, he asks, "Should we go back inside?" But after asking the question, his phone buzzed. Upon looking at it, Exton frowns. He had opened a text message from Jae, "This mother –"

"What?" Alannah says, turning to place her feet flat on the deck's floor.

"They left."

"Who left?"

"Jae and your girl."

Alannah stands. "Seriously?"

"Yeah. I just got a text from Jae. Told me he would pay for me to get a ride back."

Storming inside, Alannah calls out Sherrie's name. Frustrated, she yells, "SHERRIE! SHERRIE!" She goes into the room where they once were. Only, she notices the room was empty. Same for the other rooms nearby. However, Alannah still searches for Sherrie as if she was looking for a lost child. In the back of her mind, Sherrie was still in the home somewhere being naughty.

"They left, Alannah," Exton says, watching Alannah move about the hallways in the house aggressively.

"Why would she do that? Just leave like that?"

"It's okay."

"It's not okay," Alannah says, walking back to her phone. Grabbing it, she uses her finger to do a couple clicks and opens the text from Sherrie. Shaking her head, she says, "I can't believe this chick. Leaving me here with you," Her fingers moving rapidly. Alannah texts something back.

Exton approaches Alannah slowly. "Do you want me to leave?"

Alannah inhales and exhales heavily. "Leave how? They left you."

"I can get a ride."

Alannah doesn't respond, shaking her head subtly.

"How about we just continue our conversation on the couch? We were starting to have fun, right? Right?"

Alannah sighs, still shocked Sherrie would leave. She walks away without saying anything, sitting on the couch frustrated.

Exton follows, sitting next to her closely. He rubs her back to ease Alannah's nerves and the situation. Unable to sit still, Alannah gets up and paces.

This chick, she thinks aloud.

Chapter 24

AWAKENING SLOWLY, LINCOLN WAS STARTLED BY A police patrol car that zooms by. He was almost certain that where he was parked was only for police surveillance. With several empty bottles of liquor on the seat and the floor of his car, Lincoln believed he would be arrested were he caught sitting in this location.

Sitting up, Lincoln noticed several missed calls and texts from Zeke and Tommy. Putting his phone away, he refocuses on the house. Rain is coming down heavier, making it even harder to see. It's getting colder outside, causing his windows to fog. But he can see two people moving inside the home.

Who left? Did they leave and come back? He thinks. Pressing the start button to deactivate the car's engine, Lincoln watches the two people move throughout the home. He debates on leaving, especially with the police driving by.

Nah, he thinks. Grabbing all the bottles in the car, and drinking the last bottle quickly, Lincoln puts them back in the bag they once were. Then, he gets out of the car. He throws on his hood to block the rain, and darts across the street where he moves down the road toward the home. He can't see much from where he is. Though he remembers that most of the back and sides of the home were made of windows.

Approaching the left side of the home, Lincoln stops at the tall security fence that wrapped around the entire estate. The fence had to be about eight-feet tall. Getting over the fence wasn't a problem. *But what if there was a security sensor? A home like this must have an advanced security system*, he thinks. He doesn't want to trip any alarms.

Running toward the rear corner of the fence to get a better look inside, Lincoln dips down a hill along a sparse tree line. Large stones were scattered amongst the trees. The size of the land and the dips makes him feel as if he is running through an obstacle course. Reaching a hill which has a clear view toward the rear of the home, he paused and looked around, hiding behind a tree.

The area around the home was peaceful and quiet apart from the growing storm. Something about being between the trees and hilly, grassy area spoke to Lincoln's soul. The sound of the thunder and the feel of the rain calmed him for a moment. He was fascinated by the home and the land. It was the perfect lifestyle he had always wanted to give Alannah. He had wanted this type of homelife. For the first time, he felt something within him that gave him hope. Once he got his woman back, he would pursue something better. He would fix their broken relationship. The feeling was sobering. But first, he had to get his woman back.

His phone goes off again. His father was calling. After looking at it quickly, he turns it off. Now that he can get a better look inside, Lincoln can almost clearly see Alannah pacing back and forth near the kitchen. She was talking to someone, but the person was not in Lincoln's view. They were blocked by a wall or column. He wondered if she was talking to the SINC. More than likely she was. Just the thought of Alannah being with a robot disgusted Lincoln more, causing him to become angry again.

He continues watching from his vantage point, plotting his next move. He thinks about the gun that he should bought weeks ago. For some reason he feels he needs it now. Then the sounds of nature begin to bother him, since the storm is creating complete darkness outside. The wind has picked up, moving the trees more. Storm clouds have grown larger and thicker. Lightning strikes in the distance, prompting Lincoln to decide soon.

Glancing to his side, Lincoln noticed the same police car returning down the road. Another set of random lights seem to be moving along a hill. They appear at the closest home about a quarter mile away. Lincoln takes a deep breath. At this point, he is committed to getting inside and confronting his woman.

Moving closer to the fence, he eyes the corners of the home's interior. Lincoln looks for any cameras or other security devices. From what he can tell, he doesn't notice anything remotely resembling a security device. But that doesn't mean they aren't present. Leaping to grab the top of the fence, Lincoln can't get a good grip on the water-soaked railing. After multiple attempts, he manages to grip the railing and get his forearm level atop of it. At this point, he can pull himself up and sling his leg across the rail. Lincoln then slides down the other side.

Crouching, Lincoln claps loudly two times but then waits quietly. Nothing. He claps loudly again and several more times. Still, nothing. *If there were sound-activated, security devices, they would have come on. No guard dogs*, he thinks. Locating a few small rocks near his feet, Lincoln grabs them. He holds them in the palm of his hand. With the other hand, he threw them one-by-one toward the home.

The first rock landed just at the foot of the deck steps. Yet, there was not any response from the believed- to-be hidden security system. Throwing the second rock a little harder, this one landed on the deck and bounced a bit. Nothing. Throwing the last one even harder, the rock hit the glass hard enough to cause a sound. But still, no response from a security system.

Inside, Alannah paused her pacing to sit back down next to Exton. His touch was becoming soothing. As soon as she calmed down, she heard the sound from the glass in the kitchen.

"What was that?" Alannah says, jerking away from Exton's touch.

"I don't know," Without moving, Exton stared at the path leading to the kitchen. He looks back at Alannah.

Alannah, wide-eyed and stunned Exton didn't leap to inspect the area from which the sound came, says, "Well can you go check?"

Clearing his throat, Exton replies, "Uh, okay. Yeah." Exton hesitantly rises to his feet, glancing at Alannah. He then makes his way awkwardly toward the kitchen, cautiously looking around.

"What are you . . . scared?" Alannah asks, impatiently.

Exton shakes his head. "Nah. Nah. I'm good."

Lincoln patiently waits to see if his last attempt of alerting someone in the house worked. Moments later, he can see what appeared to be a man walking toward the rear door. Oddly, the man looks out of the window.

There it is. Fuckin' robot, Lincoln thinks.

"I don't see anything!" Exton shouts, leaning and stretching his neck to see out of the windows. He activates one of the lights that shine above the deck. "Must've just been a tree branch or something . . . hitting the house."

Upon the lights being activated, Lincoln notices security cameras near the rear doors. One was positioned in a corner above the main level door and lead into the kitchen from the deck. The other was positioned above the door leading to the basement and down some steps.

By this point, rain was heavily falling. It made it even harder to see. Lightning struck in the distance. It was time for Lincoln to move closer. Lincoln hoped that the rain would distort the camera's view, the same way it had distorted the view through the glass windows.

Maneuvering down the side of the fence and staying low, he first approached the basement level door and stood beneath the camera. Placing his hand on the back of the camera, he turns it gently to face the wall.

Inside of the home, the camera view changes on the security console. But Alannah is away from the console and too busy to notice.

Lincoln presses against the basement door, turning the handle. Unsurprisingly, it was locked. So, he glances around for anything usable that could be used to break the handle or the long strips of abstract-designed glass in its center. When he cannot find anything, Lincoln changes his mind. He moves up the stairs and tries the door by the deck, which leads to the main level and kitchen. Maybe it was left unlocked.

Even though he ran up the stairs lightly, Lincoln almost falls because of the rain-soaked steps. His body makes a thump sound. Lincoln hopes it doesn't alert the SINC or anyone else. Quickly he crawls to a nearby corner, peeking his head out every so often while waiting to see if anyone returns.

Inside of the home, Exton has returned to the couch beside Alannah. He has refilled her glass with wine, and gently rubs her back as she drinks. Neither say much as Alannah does her best to forget her frustration. This becomes easier with the more Exton touches her.

Lifting her shirt from behind, Exton moves his massage from atop her clothing to touching her skin. The feel of his fingers on her lower back sends a chill over Alannah's body, causing her to jerk.

"You good?" Exton asks.

Alannah giggles at the goosebumps which have quickly appeared across her arms. She hasn't felt this aroused in a while and being tipsy is amplifying the experience. "Sorry, I – I ... Nothing."

Lightning strikes again. This time, it's close enough to the home that it causes the power to go out. All the lights inside and outside turn off abruptly, startling everyone.

"Oh shit!" Lincoln whispers aggressively, ducking more outside.

Alannah jumps nervously, spilling some of her wine. "Damn it!"

"Let me help you," Exton says, reaching out to feel for napkins that were on the coffee table. Struggling to find them in the dark, he begins wiping Alannah down softly.

"Now I gotta find some candles."

"Shouldn't a house like this have a generator?" Exton asks, looking around.

Alannah shrugs.

Moving around the house slowly, Alannah makes her way back into the kitchen. She feels her way through drawers, using her phone as a flashlight to locate candles. Exton does the same in the other room.

"Found some!" Alannah shouts.

Lincoln listens to the muffled conversation from outside, watching the two small lights move through the darkness.

Lighting several candles, Alannah places them in clusters in different parts of the room. Returning to where she had been sitting, Alannah exhales deeply. At this point, her nerves were shot. She didn't know how to proceed with the evening or with Exton in front of her. Meanwhile, the SINC was in the other room.

Sitting awkwardly next to each other, Alannah leans over and rests her head on Exton's shoulder. He smiles at Alannah, realizing that his efforts to get her more relaxed worked enough to bring forth this moment. He begins to rub her again gently, while the flicker of the candle flames jumps around the room.

Stopping his massage, Exton puts his glass down on the floor nearby. He stands up in front of Alannah. Kneeling on one of his knees, he reaches for one of her legs.

"Um, what are you doing?" Alannah asks, hesitantly letting Exton lift her leg up.

Grabbing Alannah's foot, Exton rests it on his opposite leg. He begins to rub it sensually. "Just relax."

Alannah watches Exton over the top of her glass as she finishes her wine.

Outside, Lincoln gathers himself. The power outage froze him in place for a moment, unsure of what to do next. He approaches the main rear door in the same way as the other. Here, too, Lincoln turns the camera so that it's facing the wall. Quietly, he tip-toes to the largest available glass window to peek inside. From where he stands, he can see the silhouette of Alannah on the couch. She is holding a wine glass. One of her legs seems to be propped up, but the rest of the view is blocked by a partition wall.

Lincoln stands perfectly statuesque, watching to see what happens next. He seemingly blends in with the dark and the rain like one of the trees. Even his own reflection seems to creep him out a little when the sky brightens.

Exton's massage efforts have moved from Alannah's foot to her lower leg. After spending some time massaging this area, he moves to her other foot and does the same. Then, Exton causally makes his way up to Alannah's thigh. He continues to massage her. He moves just above her knee, gripping her soft thighs more and more. The sounds of enjoyment from Alannah are motivation enough for him to continue.

When his hands get a little too high for Alannah's liking, she grabs them and stops him. Saying nothing to this act, Exton grabs Alannah's hand and massages each finger gently. He moves onto her wrist and her forearm. Moving his body between Alannah's legs, he continues to massage her arm. He works his way to her shoulders and then her neck.

Finishing her wine, Alannah gazes at Exton. Vulnerability fills her eyes. With her mouth half-open, Alannah breathes heavily and wonders what he will do next.

Exton can feel Alannah's legs tightening around him, as if her body was telling him to do more. Without hesitation, he leans in. He tilts his head to the side, going in for another kiss. Exton practically puts his whole tongue in Alannah's mouth, kissing her aggressively.

Alannah lowers her guard completely, releasing all reasons as to why she should let Exton have his way. It was as if she was under his spell. Neither the scent of his cologne nor the wine wasn't helping. Every pore of her body is on fire while her lady parts throbbed. Her nipples fought their way through her shirt.

Furious, Lincoln had seen all that he could stand. How could Alannah not only cheat, but cheat with a SINC? It enraged him to the highest level possible. Heading back to the door, Lincoln gently turned the handle. He pushed on it, hoping it was unlocked. Hearing the latch open, Lincoln was relieved as he stepped inside the washroom near the kitchen. Soaked, the water from the rain fell from his clothing to the floor in heavy droplets.

Standing and listening for a moment, he does his best to calm his breathing. Therefore, he wouldn't be heard. Between traversing the home's terrain and hopping the fence, nervousness and now his increased anger, he didn't want to alert Alannah that he was there.

Moving to the edge of the washroom where it met the kitchen, Lincoln looked around in the slight darkness. The light from the candles only illuminated a small part of the nearby rooms. The house was so big that he wasn't sure which way through the kitchen would lead him to Alannah. He couldn't be certain that she wouldn't see him coming. The kitchen was connected to multiple hallways that looked different inside than it did through the soaked windows.

Turning down one hallway, it was clear to Lincoln that, after having walked several feet, he had gone the wrong way. He was walking further away from the light, and there were sounds of activity in the other room. But even realizing that he was walking in the wrong direction, Lincoln couldn't resist checking out some of the house. He deeply wanted to see what it was about this place that kept Alannah away, believing there was more to it.

Making a couple turns, Lincoln went down a corridor and passed a few rooms. He sniffed the air, finally smelling her fragrance after what seemed to be a long time away from her. He followed the scent toward a room, grabbing the doorknob and opening the door.

Down a hall and in another room, Alannah and Exton continue passionately kissing. So much so, that Alannah accidentally pushes her phone from off the couch and onto the floor. It causes the phone to make a thump sound.

Hearing the sound, Lincoln stops in his tracks. He doesn't enter the room. Instead, he follows the sound down another hallway. The home has a fluid design, including multiple ways to get to almost every area on the main level.

Walking as quietly as he can, Lincoln began hearing soft moaning and breathing in front of him.

"Oh, mmm. This feels . . . so good," Alannah says, moaning sensually. The warmness of her breath falling into Exton's mouth. "I – I shouldn't . . ."

"Shh," Exton kisses and licks her on her neck. "Just relax. Enjoy this feeling." Unbeknownst to him, he accidentally nudges Alannah's phone under the couch with his leg.

Lincoln is so stunned and angry by what he hears, so much in fact that he stops where he stands. Breathing slowly and deeply, he does his best to control his anger.

"Wait, wait." Alannah pushes Exton away from her gently. She tries to catch her breath.

Exton sighs frustratingly. "What's wrong, Alannah?"

Unable to speak, Alannah just shakes her head. She buries her face in her hands.

"Do you not like it? Should I do something different?" Exton says, standing.

Alannah sighs.

Just a few feet away, Lincoln can now see the activity fully through the reflection of the fireplace glass on a nearby wall.

"Would you like some water?" Exton asks.

Crying a little, Alannah nods.

"Your wish is my command." Exton walks briskly toward the kitchen, until he feels something wet on the floor. He slows down, unable to see in this darker area. *Hmph. That's strange*, he thinks aloud.

Realizing that he could be seen, Lincoln quickly backs into a nook in the dark hallway. Now that he is so close, Lincoln begins seeing red.

Returning with the water, Exton kneels in front of Alannah again and hands her the glass. Alannah takes a few sips before looking at Exton softly. Hesitantly, she pulls him in close and kisses him tenderly.

Having moved back to his original vantage point in the hallway, Lincoln watches Alannah's actions once more. Breathing heavily, he closes his eyes. Something snaps inside of him. Rage courses through his body uncontrollably. Looking around with purpose, Lincoln debates on a weapon. He is unsure of how a SINC would respond to a threat. So, he needed to choose wisely. A hand-to-hand fight with a machine didn't seem like a wise thing to do. And even if he had a gun, would it work against a SINC?

Opening the drawers in the kitchen would be loud and draw attention. Henceforth, he had to find something already out and within reach. He had to blindside the SINC at all costs. He approaches a champagne-colored, metal vase in the corner. Lifting it gently, he tests the weight to ensure he could wield it. It was heavy enough for his use for it. Lincoln does all of this while keeping an eye on the infidelity in the other room.

Reclining on the couch, Alannah lifts her legs. She wraps them around Exton's waist. Both return to kissing intensely. Alannah's phone buzzes from underneath the couch, but she is too consumed to notice the faint sound.

Working up his nerves, Lincoln breathes in and out heavily. It was as if he was readying himself before one of his high school basketball games. It was some sort of ritual to get the adrenaline going. Now holding his breath, Lincoln runs non-stop into the room where Alannah was. Running through the darkness toward Exton, Lincoln roars at the top of his lungs.

Hearing the sound and seeing the shape of a person in black, Alannah jerks back and screams loudly. At the same time, she pushes against Exton. She tries to get them both out of the way of what was coming. Before Exton can turn around fast enough, however, Lincoln raised the floor vase high. He slammed it down the back of Exton's head.

Instantly, Exton falls face-forward onto Alannah's lap. Blood pours from the back of his head, spraying in the air sporadically because of the deep, open wound. Blood travels practically everywhere; on Alannah, the couch and floor. Blood also gets onto Lincoln's face and clothing.

Lights within the home flicker as the power struggled to come back on. The glow of the candles illuminated only certain corners of the room, causing Lincoln's face to be unseen from where Alannah was sitting.

"PLEASE DON'T HURT ME!" Alannah screams.

Lincoln stands in place, breathing monstrously. He drops the vase onto the floor like a hunter who just killed a threatening, wild animal. The weight of the vase causes a loud bang to travel across the room. It only scares Alannah more. Finally, the electricity comes back on, activating everything in the house. The lights and appliances all make various sounds at once, also startling Alannah.

In the other room, the power is restored to the SINC. Because of the power outage and abrupt restoration of electricity, the SINC begins to power up. It does so without requiring Alannah's information.

Lincoln is so oddly energized that he doesn't notice the blood. He was covered in it, as if he went to war and was on the first line of his platoon.

Looking down at her hands and body, Alannah is in so much shock. She can't seem to let out another scream or say anything. The blood was everywhere. She slightly pushes Exton, causing his limp and bloody body to roll onto the couch and then onto the floor. Blood pools beneath of him.

Looking at Exton's lifeless body, Alannah curls up into a ball at the corner of the couch.

"How could you, Alannah? Why?" Lincoln asks, angrily. He removes the hood from his head. "How could you cheat on me with – with . . . wait a minute. Is that – is that . . . blood? Why is there blood, A?"

Alannah is so stunned that she can't speak at first. "Lincoln?"

"A!! Why is there blood?! Robots don't bleed!"

Her mouth shivers in fear and shock. Alannah holds her face. "You killed him. Oh my god. You KILLED HIM, LINCOLN!"

"I . . . I didn't know. I thought . . . oh shit. I thought you were with one of those things. A SINC! OH, FUCK, A!"

Alannah begins to rock, unsure on what to say or do next.

"Okay, okay. Um. Shit," Lincoln stammers, pacing for a moment in front of Exton's body. "Okay. This is what we are going to do –"

Before Lincoln can finish his statement, a loud and deep boom sound covers the area. It was as if lightning struck in the center of the room. Blood flies across Alannah's face, causing her to close her eyes quickly. The sound was loud enough that it caused Alannah to grab her head, covering her ears. She responded as if she had a horrible migraine. For a few seconds, she was unable to hear anything.

Meanwhile, Alannah's phone buzzed again from under the couch.

It was as if time froze. Events that had happened during the past few weeks flashed through Alannah's mind. Then certain events from the past few months. The good and the bad. The laughs and the tears. The smiles and the arguments.

Wiping her face slowly, Alannah looks up at Lincoln. His facial expression had gone blank, as if someone had sucked the air out of his body. He was confused as to why.

Grabbing at his chest, Lincoln looks down at the blood. It was all over his hand, and there was a sizable hole in his stomach. "Alannah," he says, struggling to breathe now. Gasping for air, he falls to his knees slowly. "Alannah."

Wide-eyed, Alannah realizes that Lincoln had been shot. Screaming, she leaps to her feet and jumps over Exton's body toward Lincoln.

Standing a few feet away is the awkward neighbor, holding a shotgun that was still pointed in the direction where Lincoln once stood. A string of smoke left the barrel of the gun. The neighbor was shaking, having shocked himself emotionally by the shooting.

"I, I, I . . . I didn't want to shoot him. I didn't want to. I promise I didn't."

"Oh my god," Alannah says, shivering.

"I . . . I was driving my four-wheeler behind the house looking to get some wood. Didn't know how bad this storm was going to be. Sometimes the power will be out for a while. My plan was to come to check on you after I got enough pieces. I saw . . . I saw – oh shit. Man, I didn't want to shoot him." The awkward neighbor lowers the gun, grabbing his brow with his opposite hand. "I saw him sneak in the house. Please tell me he was a burglar."

Alannah remains in shock, staring at Lincoln.

"When I saw him lurking, I returned for my gun. OH MAN!"

Cradling Lincoln's head like a baby, Alannah rocks from side to side and cries. It was as if the neighbor was talking to a wall. Alannah couldn't see or hear anything but Lincoln in front of her now. As Lincoln's breathing gets worse, she kisses Lincoln on his forehead multiple times.

"I'm – I'm – I'm sorry . . . baby. I . . . I just –" Lincoln struggles to speak, gurgling blood.

"Shh, shh, shh. I know, baby. I know. I'm so sorry." Alannah turns toward the neighbor. "GO GET SOME FUCKIN' HELP!"

Alannah's phone buzzes one last time from underneath the couch. The activity in the room makes it much more challenging for Alannah to notice it. The buzz was an alert from Chase. He had sent Alannah a text message regarding her work situation.

ALANNAH! GOT GOOD NEWS FOR YOU! LETS PARTY THIS WEEKEND! 7PM SATURDAY AT MY HOUSE! KAREN IS COOKING! AS ALWAYS, BRING LINCOLN! YEP! THE NEWS IS THAT GOOD!

Alannah's tone startles the awkward neighbor, causing him to run out of the front door quickly.

As Alannah cradles Lincoln, a slow but steady sound of footsteps travels down the adjacent hallway. Looking up, Alannah is curious but aware as to what the sound could be. Her gaze is met by the presence of the SINC, standing at the threshold between the rooms.

"Is everything okay, Alannah?"

Furious by the SINC's presence, Alannah screams, "GET OUT! GET THE FUCK OUT!"

Unsure on how to respond, the SINC stands still. It moves its head perplexingly, as if it had been abruptly recoded and was provided a foreign command.

Alannah watches as Lincoln's eyes seem to change. He takes his final few breaths. She cries uncontrollably, resting her head on his.

Moments later, Sherrie returns to the house with Jae. She felt bad for leaving Alannah alone the way she did. It took her a while to get back to the house, because of the storm and some fallen trees on the road not too far away. Pulling up to the house, she noticed a man running aggressively from the property.

"Who was that?" Jae asks.

Sherrie looks around curiously. "I have no idea."

Letting herself through the house's front gate, she parked her car and gets out. She walked toward the front door that was already slightly opened.

Jae scratches his head. "Why is the door open?"

"Hmm. That's odd." Sherrie says, pushing the door more and walking into the foyer. "Hello? Alannah?"

Moments later, red and blue lights begin to blink in the distance. They become more prominent as the police begin to arrive from various directions. Even though the neighbor gotten a hold of them quickly, they were delayed in responding because of the storm. But there were a few patrol cars already nearby.

As they arrive and exit their cars, a loud scream could be heard coming from the home. Drawing their guns, each one of the officers - including a new, special *Security* Integrated Neuro-Robotic Companion - enters the home.

Outside, several officers sweep the perimeter. One notices a trash can that had a bag partly exposed inside of it. Curious, the officer puts on rubber gloves, opens the can, and retrieves the bag. Cautiously opening the bag, they find a note inside of it with a revolver handgun. The note reads:

This home isn't safe. Please be careful.

Other available works by C. Schmidt:

Hock City *(ISBN 978-0692121030)*

Uhmandra *(ISBN 978-0578613383)*

Hakra *(ISBN 978-0578891163)*